THE OTHER KEY

AN OTHER WORLD NOVEL

C. A. VARIAN

The Other Key

Book Cover, Maps, and Formatting by by Blurbs and Baubles

Chapter Header and Line Break by Leigh Cadiente

Editing by Willow Oak Author Services

Page edge design by Painted Wings Publishing Services

Trigger Warning

There are mature themes throughout this book, and it is not intended for readers under 17 years of age.

The following themes are explored in The Other Key: Graphic (consensual) sexual content, terminal illness/contemplating death, captivity, slavery, abduction, talks of rape, torture, sex trafficking, vulgar language, and murder.

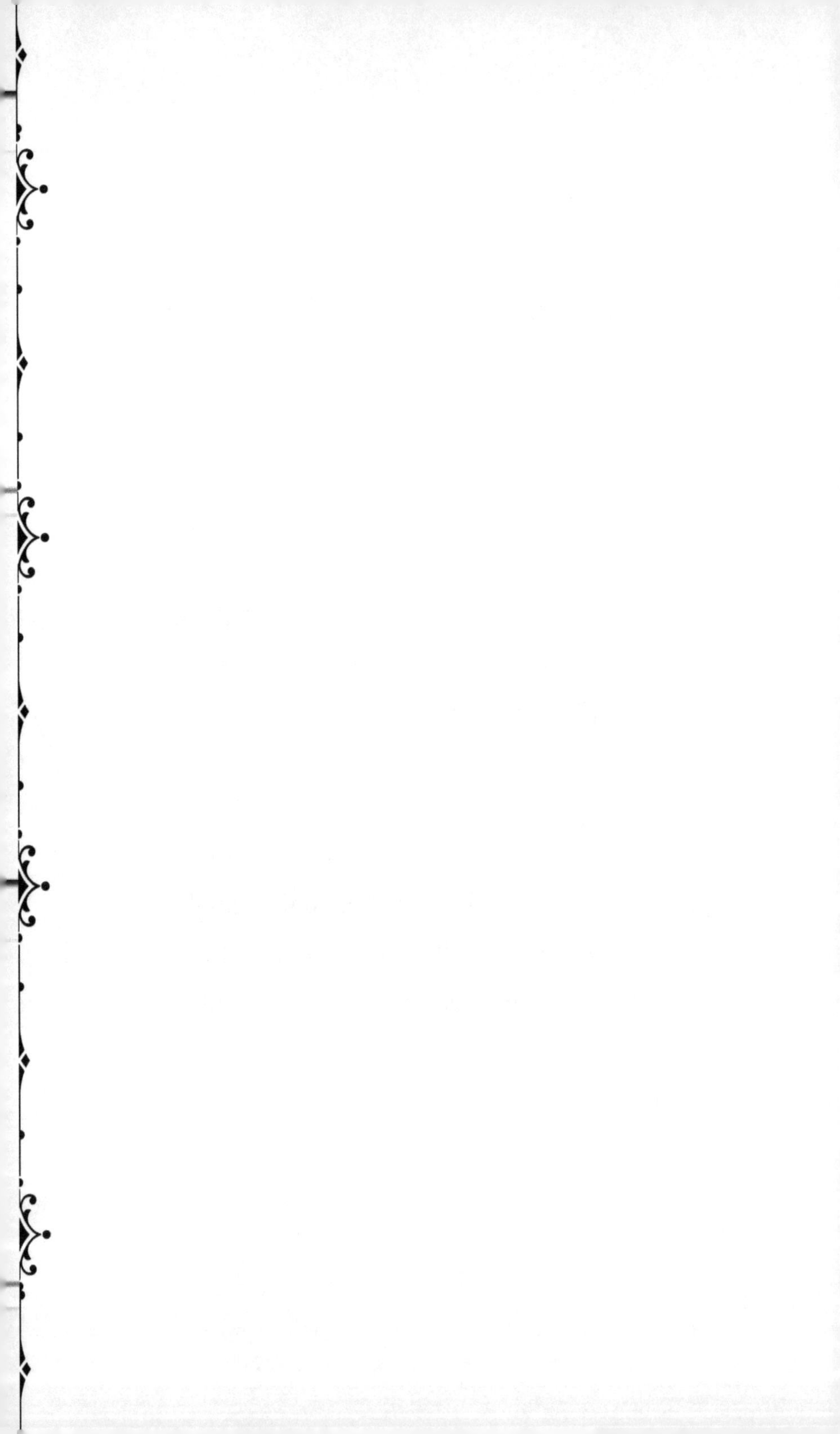

ECROMOS

EMERALD SEA
COURT
OF
KNOWLEDGE
CLOUDFELL
WHISPERING FOREST
PORTAL
COURT
OF
HARMONY
COURT
OF
COURAGE
COURT
OF
CHAOS

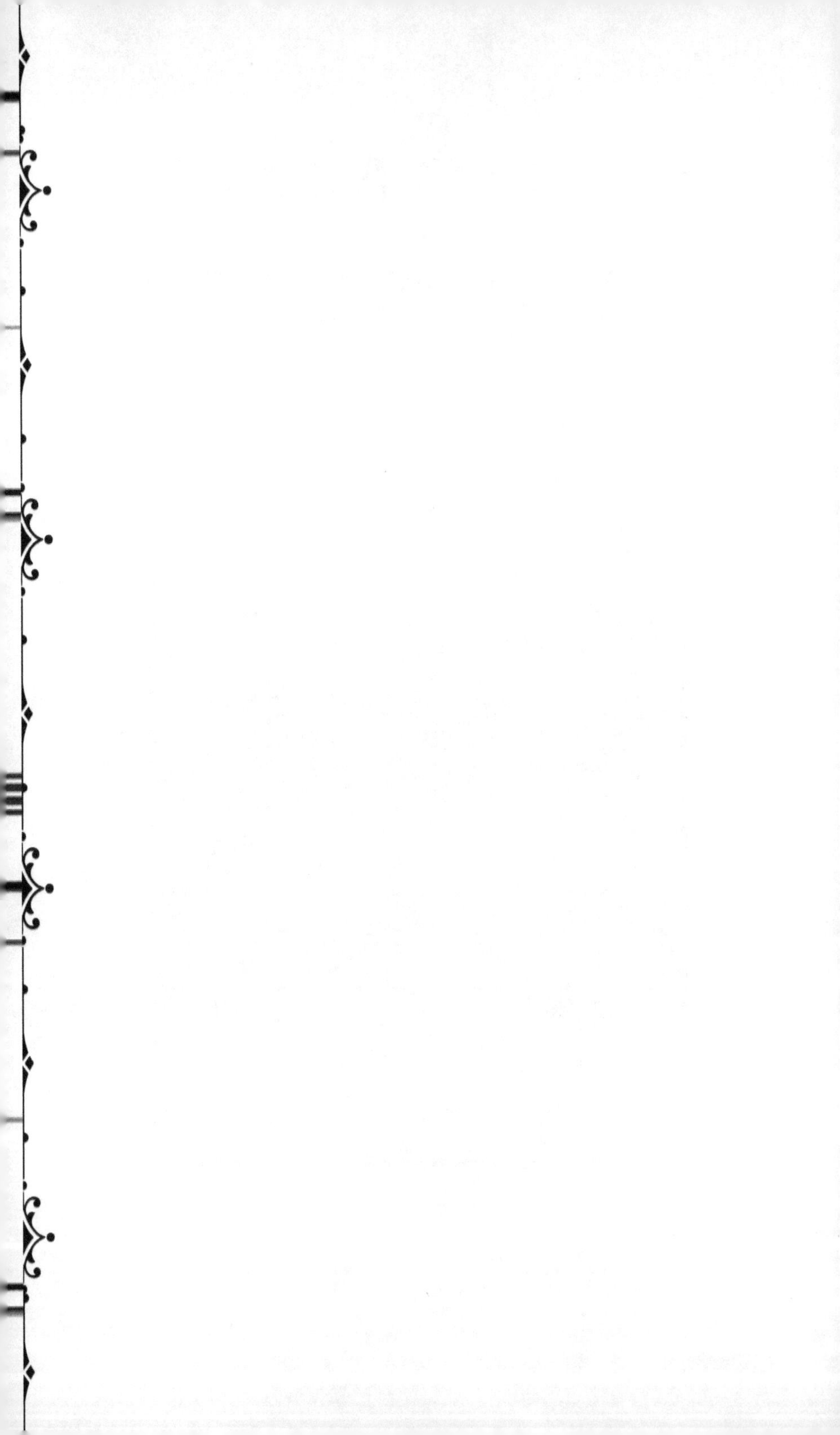

Contents

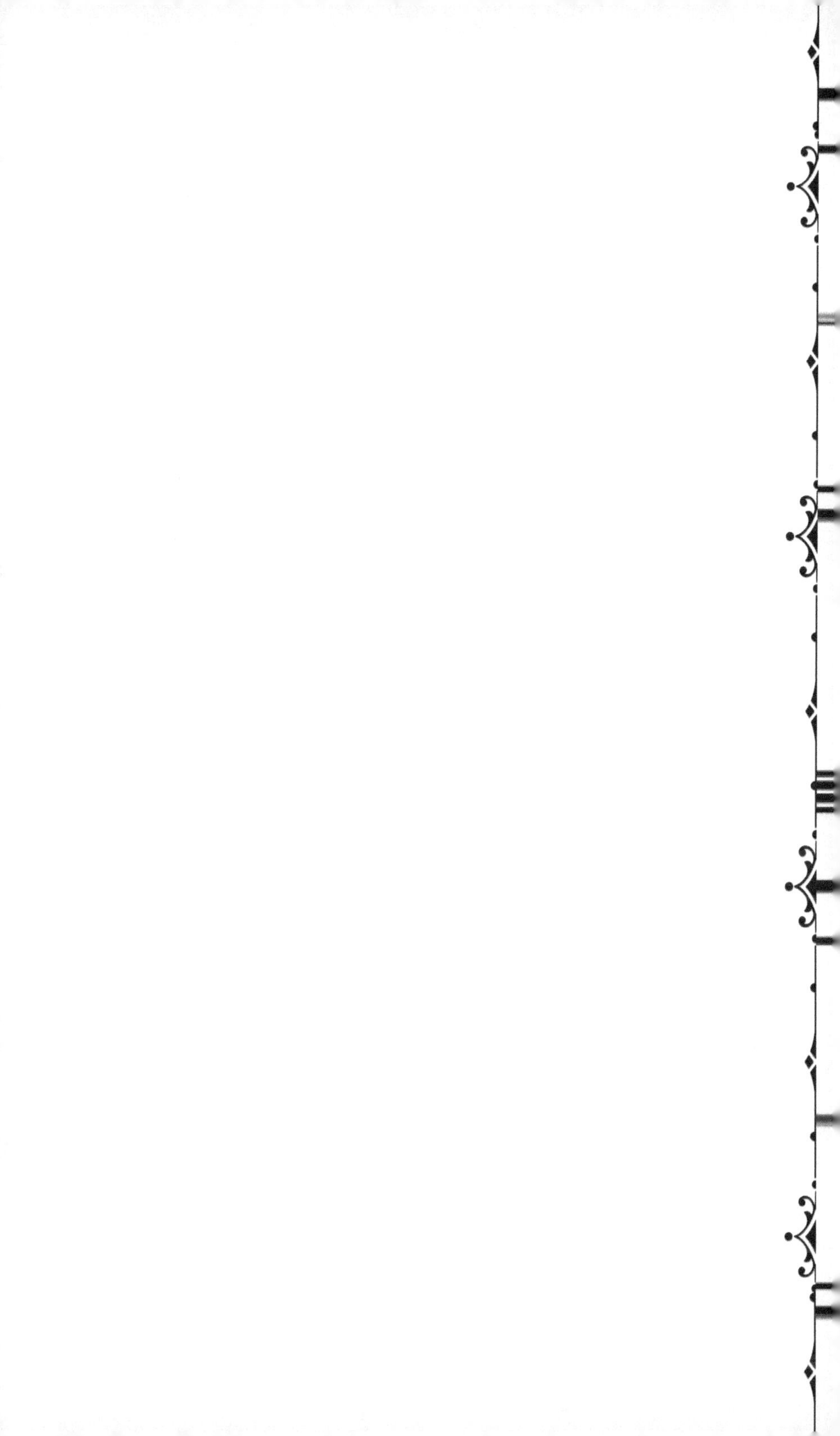

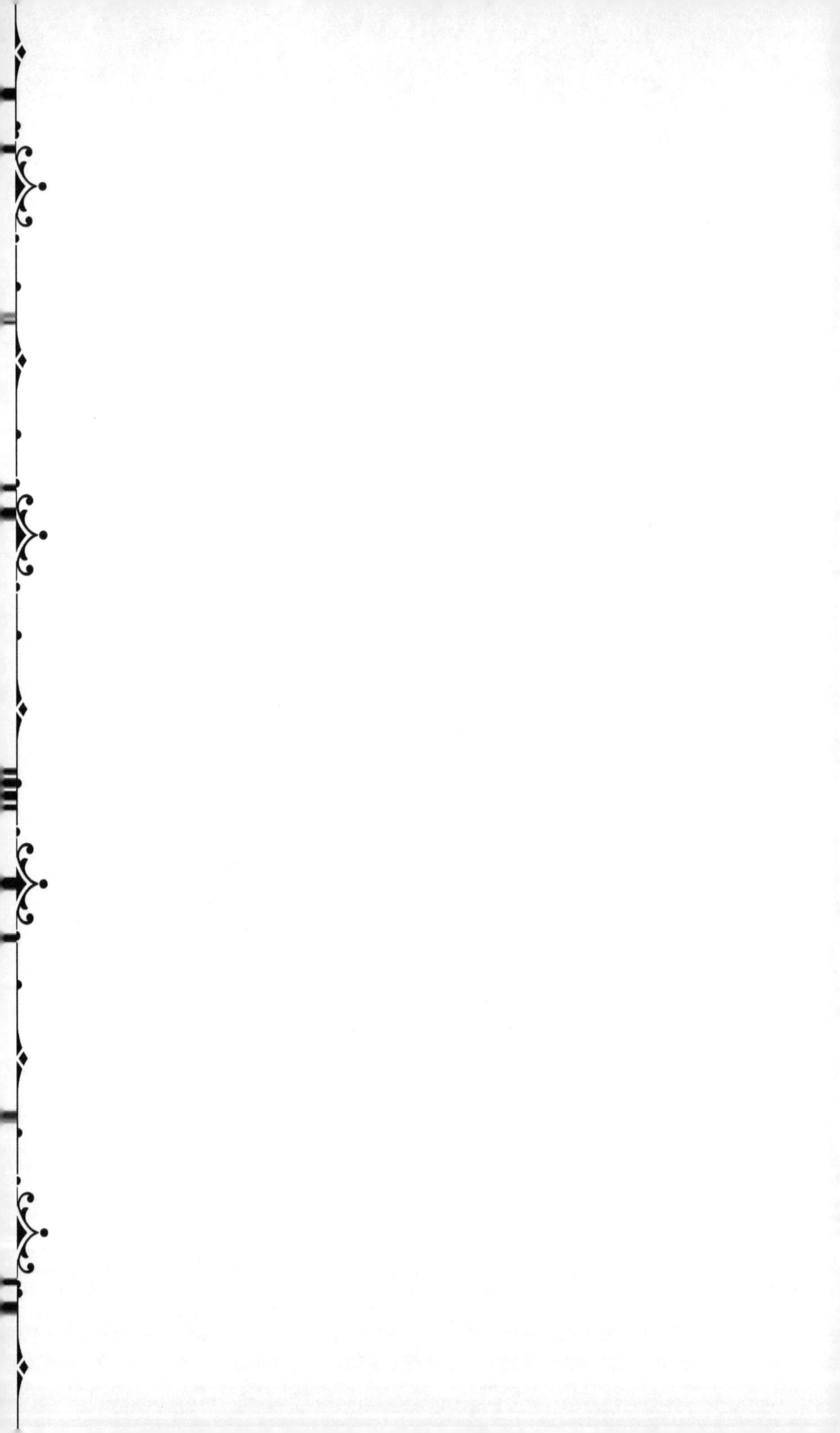

Prior to using the key of Ecromos, which allowed Zoe Lawson to cross over into the fae realm, she had given up on life, and become resigned to the brain cancer that had taken everything from her for so long. From the time she was a teenager, she had been suffering from a brain tumor. It had never been possible for her to live a life like other teenagers, or like any other twenty-something.

When all her hair had to be shaved off or fell out by itself, regardless of how beautiful she was, there were few men knocking at her door to be with her. The key of the Ecromos, however, represented the chance to start over. In the fae world she could find hope.

Zoe never forgot the day she received the enchanted golden key. It was a Tuesday. Following lunch with her friend Jessica, they went to see her cancer specialist in the city. It had never occurred to her until she saw the look on his face as he read the scan reports that she had become terminal. With maybe a year to live, the doctor gave her the golden key and explained how it worked as well as he could. She thanked him politely and left the room in a daze, clutching the enchanted key tightly in her hand. As she stepped out of the building, she felt the warm sun on her face and a flood of emotions swelled up inside her. She knew that her life was about to change forever, but for better or worse, she wasn't sure.

The keys of Ecromos were typically given to terminally ill human women who were of childbearing age. The keys allowed those women, if they chose, to cross through a portal and enter the fae realm of Ecromos. There was less understanding of what those women were expected to do once they arrived. Since no one had been allowed back through the door, no one knew exactly what happened on the other side.

As far as Zoe knew, and as far as the doctors and the government knew, the women might have been crossing into the fae realm to be put down.

Rumors abounded, however. Among the most common rumors was that once the women reached the other world, a male- a fated mate, so to speak-was waiting for them with a key that was identical to theirs. As soon as the magical keys were reunited, the human woman and the fae male would have babies and live happily ever after. In this way, they would help to repopulate a world that was lacking in women and children. This rumor of a fated mate and a magical key that reunited two worlds was something that the women could cling to, giving them hope and a purpose in their journey.

There were also rumors that human women were sold off on sex trafficking markets to the highest bidders. Those males would have children with the humans who crossed into Ecromos, because the realm did not have enough females or children. These rumors claimed that women were bred like livestock and had no freedom. As a result of these unknowns, Zoe was too afraid to use her key until it was almost too late. Zoe feared that if she opened the door with her key, she could be facing a life of enslavement and loss of her own autonomy- a fate worse than death. So, she set the key on the table beside her bed and left it there.

Only a few months after receiving her key, her health began to decline rapidly. In no time at all, she was in hospice and fighting for her life every single day. In the absence of family, a significant other, and friends, it had been the loneliest time of her life.

Her friend Jessica came to visit her one day and they talked about the key. After putting the rumors aside and taking the leap of faith to save her own life, she decided to try to cross the portal and become part fae, knowing she would be cured once she did. Jessica drove her into the mountains where the temple that housed the portal was, and then rolled her in a wheelchair into the building and through the door.

She was captured before she had even taken a step away from the portal through which she could not return.

The male who captured her was Lord Argall. The aristocrat was a very wealthy member of the Court of Knowledge. While she didn't know for sure, she was convinced he had the support of the king to steal women and sell them as sex slaves.

After spending some time at Lord Argall's manor, she discovered the story about fated mates was true, but then learned that her own mate would be unable to locate her.

When the Lord's people picked her up from the portal, the first thing they did was hide her key in a box that blocked magic. That was what he did with all the women's keys. Their mates could not find them if their keys could not sense one another.

So, Zoe worked in the brothel nearly every day for a year until a young woman named Elianna arrived. Elianna had been stolen also.

What no one realized until later was that when the powerful fae healer cured Elianna of her cancer, she pushed some of her own power into Elianna- a *lot* of power.

Fortunately, the healer, who was also their caretaker at the manor, was on their side. Shortly after Elianna arrived, the healer returned Elianna's key, allowing her mate to finally locate her. Since Zoe was friends with Elianna and was with Elianna when her mate rescued her, she escaped with them.

Taking to horseback, the three fled into the forest, knowing the Lord's men were chasing them. Having run and hidden for a while, they were almost out of the Court of Knowledge, out of the area where the Lord could look for them, when they had stopped to camp, and Zoe had been re-captured.

This is where the story picks up...

Chapter 1

Cailean

Drenched in sap from being tied to a tree, Cailean darted forward as his brother, father, Blaze, and Elianna kept the guards occupied. His one goal was to rescue Zoe, the human female Lord Argall's guards had abducted, and get her to safety. Besides knowing how she'd left her home world to seek a cure for her terminal illness, and that she'd been taken from the portal by those intending to trade her as a slave before meeting her fated mate, he didn't know much about her. During their ride through the Whispering Forest together on his mare, they talked a little, but not much. It had been difficult for them to talk with each other due to the slaver's guards searching for them.

As the blond female lay unconscious in the tent, Cailean scooped her up in his arms and fled into the forest, leaving the makeshift camp and the others behind them. As he ran through the forest, Zoe was like a feather in his arms, but he worried that she hadn't awoken. While he and Blaze were tied to a tree, he had been able to see her unmoving form as the lord's guard watched over her in the tent, they'd kept her in. While he was unsure of what potion or magic, they had used on her, she had been unconscious for at least three hours. He had to get her to safety and find a way to wake her up. If he didn't, her life could be at risk.

Once they arrived back where he and his brother had secured their horses, Cailean set Zoe down on the ground next to his mare, Wallflower. He smoothed the human's long hair away from her face, projecting all the fae power he could into her sleeping form.

"*Please* wake up, Zoe."

It would only be a matter of moments before they had to mount the horse and continue toward the Court of Harmony, where he hoped to meet the others. After everything they'd been through to save her, he couldn't risk them being captured again if they stayed idle for too long.

Smoothing the cool water from his canteen down her cheeks, he pleaded with her to wake up. After a few minutes, his efforts paid off when Zoe started to stir, her eyes fluttering as she groaned. She slowly opened her eyes, confusion and fear etched on her face.

"There you go, sunshine. You're safe."

Although they'd only just met, Zoe reminded him of the brilliant rays of the sun, so she'd earned the nickname right away. Her beautiful face lit up with a grin, even though she was groggy.

"Cailean? What happened?"

Knowing she was probably hungry and thirsty, he lifted the canteen to her mouth. She drank so quickly that the water dribbled down her chin. With a gentle hand, he wiped the droplets away, his eyes never leaving hers.

"We saved you from Lord Argall's guards, but we have to get out of here as soon as possible. Blaze told me to grab you and flee. The others will catch up with us." Rising to his feet, Cailean reached a hand down to her, smiling when she turned her brilliant blue eyes in his direction. "Can you stand?"

She nodded. A surge of awareness flooded his system when her hand touched his, and it filled him with sadness. Although they'd both been given a key connecting them to their fated mates, hers flickered with life for someone else, as his key remained dark in his pocket. He felt something for her without a doubt, but they were destined for someone else, and that knowledge hurt him. Her mate was searching for her; the flicker of her key made that clear, but they didn't know who the male was, or *where* he was.

For as long as Cailean had been waiting for a mate in a world without enough females, he didn't know if his human mate had ever crossed into his world. He also didn't know if she would ever choose to do so. There had been many nights where he'd begged his mate to come to him through his key, but still it remained silent. Zoe, however, was in front of him, and she was gorgeous. Having her around was like a breath of fresh air, and he would have given anything for their keys to flicker for each other. He knew it was a long shot, but he still could not help but hope that Zoe might be the one to bring his key to life. Even so, he felt grateful for her presence, for the mere sight of her was enough to make him feel alive for the first time in a long time.

Although grief filled him to the brim, he supported Zoe's weight as she struggled onto her shaky legs. In an effort to steady her, he pulled her close to him, only to back away when the sensation brought by her close proximity became too overwhelming.

"Are you all right?"

Despite her wide-eyed question, he only nodded, grasping her waist and lifting her onto Wallflower.

"Don't worry about me. It is you who just suffered through an ordeal."

Settling on the saddle with Zoe's back to his chest, Cailean clenched his jaw and urged Wallflower forward. Eventually, Zoe's mate would come for her, and he would have to let her go. Even though he knew she had never been his, to have a female unmated in his grasp, one who was everything he wanted and who seemed interested in him too, and not be able to make her his seemed like a crime against nature. Though his key was silent, his heart, body, and mind were not, making him wonder which mattered more.

Since there could have been guards anywhere looking to recapture her, Cailean and Zoe traveled for hours in relative silence. As the journey progressed, she fell asleep again, leaving only the wildlife to keep him company.

"You feel it too."

While listening for danger, he'd been so absorbed in the sounds of skittering animals and bird calls that he jumped as Zoe's voice broke the silence. He hadn't even noticed she had awoken because she was leaning against his chest so still.

"Feel what, sunshine?"

When she looked up at him, the way wisps of blond hair framed her face took his breath away.

"The electricity when we touch. Even though our keys don't recognize each other, I know you feel it as well."

Despite being right, Cailean considered lying. He didn't want there to be any doubt about who she should be with when her mate came for her. Ultimately, he just wanted her to be happy, but the selfish part of him won out. There was no way he could deny the truth to either of them.

Blowing out a breath, he nodded. "I do, but it could be nothing. Perhaps it's just what the body does when it's lonely or when it needs love."

Cailean squeezed the reins tighter to prevent his hands from touching her. There was no doubt in his mind that the last statement he made was a lie. He may have been lonely, and starved of affection, but he knew it was more than that. They both did.

Huffing out a breath, Zoe's full lips fell into a frown before she turned to look ahead. "You don't truly believe that."

Ignoring his self-control, the only part of him trying to protect his heart from getting shattered, Cailean let go of the reins with one of his hands and wrapped his arm around her waist, pulling her into him. In his heart, he struggled between the pleasure of touching her and the pain of knowing she could never be his, but the disappointment in her tone forced him to comfort her.

"My beliefs are irrelevant, Zoe. My key is silent. You are someone else's mate, and I cannot take that away from you. You will love your mate no matter who he is. It's fate, so it can't be wrong."

The words were crushing as they left his lips. Even as he said them, they felt wrong.

In part, Cailean hoped Zoe's mate would never find them. If that happened, he wondered if she would want to join him when he went back to his own home in the Court of Courage. He wondered if they could choose each other and ignore their keys altogether, but he knew he couldn't abandon his mate if she came into his realm.

Unlike the fae males who received their keys, the human women who entered their world for a cure and a mate had neither a family nor a home to return to. When they entered Ecromos, they were completely helpless, which made them easy prey for slavers who snatched them before their mates could get to them. In the event that his mate came to Ecromos, he would have to protect her even if he had no desire to be with her. Since she would have no one else to turn to, he would have to take responsibility and protect her. It would be his responsibility to ensure that she was safe from the slavers' clutches. It was a burden he had to bear.

Zoe shifted in the saddle and Cailean returned his hand to the reins, unable to touch her any longer. "Do you think the others made it? How do we know if they are coming?"

"We don't, but I've left a trail for them to follow if they did. The only thing we can do once we reach the Court of Harmony is wait. We'll find a tavern on the main road and wait there for a few days if necessary. If they don't show up..." Although the thought of losing his brother and father tore at his chest, Cailean shrugged. "Well... we'll figure out what to do then."

Glancing up to look at him, a sweet smile spread across Zoe's face as her hand slid over his again. "I told you a little about me on our first ride together, Cailean, but you are still a bit of a tall, dark, and handsome mystery to me."

Her flirty words sent a warm flush to his cheeks as a chuckle rumbled out of him. "What do you want to know? And I don't know that much about you."

She twisted in the saddle, her smile only growing as he got lost in her blue eyes. Although he knew they should be quiet so as not to draw attention, he couldn't help himself. He wanted to talk to her.

Lifting her fingers to cup her chin, she hummed as she thought of a question.

"Should I be afraid?" he asked, wrapping an arm around her back when Wallflower stepped over a fallen branch.

"Well I know you're not mated, but do you still live with your parents?" Her eyes narrowed on him as though he would lie.

"No. I do not live with my parents, but I do live near them. I have a small cottage on a portion of their property. It's a big property, though, so I have my privacy."

Taking a moment to scan the surroundings for anyone who may have approached, Cailean went silent.

"Okay, Zoe, do I get to ask a question now?"

She nodded with no hesitation, the smile on her face never falling.

"What made you decide to leave your world—if you want to talk about it? There's no pressure if you don't want to."

Although he expected her smile to fall, knowing what usually caused females to leave the human world to come to Ecromos, it didn't. "I had cancer in my brain. I was really sick, dying."

She shrugged, her eyes going distant as her face finally fell into something more subdued. The change in her emotions made him regret asking her the question. He hated to make her dredge up something painful, even if he did want to know.

"It wasn't an easy decision for me to make, and I waited until the last minute to do it. Once they put me in hospice, I felt like I couldn't wait any longer. My time was running out."

Just thinking about what would've happened to her if she hadn't come to Ecromos and received a cure chilled Cailean's blood. He lifted his arm to rub her back, if only to show her support, but the touch of his skin against hers pulsed through his body. The need to claim her as his mate continued to grow stronger, more impossible to deny.

Chapter 2

Zoe

They rode for a few more hours in relative silence but Zoe's heavy head didn't really mind. Cailean's words, his dismissal of what was between them, had wounded her somewhere deep down, even if she didn't want to admit it. The golden key still pulsed in her pocket, but she did her best to ignore the power it emanated.

For Elianna, finding her fated mate had been everything, but for Zoe it wasn't, not really. After having been a slave, forced to work in the brothel for nearly a year, all Zoe wanted was the power of choice. She wanted love like Elianna and Blaze had, but she wanted to be the one to decide what male she spent forever with. When Cailean touched her, her body told her to choose him, even if their keys didn't agree.

"And if no one shows up? If our friends don't show up and the male who my key calls to doesn't...then what? What will happen to me?"

Although Cailean stiffened behind her, it was a question she needed to ask. There was no way for her to get back to her world, not that she wanted to go back. Lord Argall's manor had been her home ever since she'd arrived in Ecromos. She had nowhere else to go if her destiny fell through.

"If your mate doesn't show up, then I'll take you home with me, of course," Cailean responded, the words filling Zoe with warmth. "I wouldn't abandon you, Zoe."

Sliding her hand onto his where he held the horse's reins as though his life depended on it, she pulled his hand away, interlacing their fingers and setting their hands on her thigh.

"That's what I hoped you would say."

He leaned closer into her as he spoke into her ear. "Regardless of what our keys say, Zoe, I would never leave you anywhere alone, or anywhere you didn't want to be. Please don't ever worry about that. You'll always have a place with me if you want or need one."

His declaration certainly released some of the stress weighing on her shoulders, but she knew it wasn't that simple. "And what about if your fated mate shows up? Surely you wouldn't be able to keep me in your home and her as well."

Although his jaw tightened, she could tell he was trying to mute his reaction so as not to worry her. "The last time my key truly sensed her was about a year ago. At this point, I've come to expect the worst and no longer believe she will come to my world. I keep the key with me just in case, but I fear she has since died."

A town surrounded by pastures and fields of flowers came into view as the trees of the Whispering Forest thinned, relief filling Zoe at the knowledge that they were no longer in Lord Argall's court. Cailean had already told her it was considered an act of war to enter a foreign court and take a female. As high ranking as Lord Argall was, he wouldn't dare to enter the Court of Harmony to steal them back- at least they hoped he wouldn't.

After he'd admitted to believing his mate had died, Zoe didn't know how to respond. Of course, she'd told him not to think that way, and squeezed his hand, but even she realized he was probably right. Either his mate had died and never come to Ecromos, or she was one of the women who'd been stolen and had their key taken away. Either scenario filled her with emotions she wasn't ready to tackle so she'd gone quiet for a while.

"Have you ever been here before? The town, I mean," she asked as she admired the fields of wildflowers on the side of the dirt road they traveled on.

Even as unsure as they were about the future of their relationship, or if there could ever be one, Cailean's hand was still on her thigh as they approached the Clumsy Weasel Tavern. She stifled a giggle at the sign that had a rodent downing a cup of ale engraved into it. Fae really were clever when naming their businesses.

"I've ridden through these small towns in the Court of Harmony a few times, but I don't think I've ever stayed at this tavern."

A stable hand walked toward them as they stopped in front of the tavern, taking the reins from Cailean so he could dismount. Once he was off the horse, he grasped Zoe around the waist, lifting her and setting her on the ground next to him.

Still early in the day, the sun was high in the sky, but Zoe couldn't help but to yawn. They'd traveled the entire night. Although she'd dozed off a few times, Cailean hadn't, so she knew she wasn't the only one who needed rest. Grabbing their bags from the saddle, Cailean placed his hand on the small of her back, leading her inside the tavern as the stable hand escorted Wallflower away.

They entered the multi-level log structure, Cailean setting their belongings down at one of the tables and then approaching the bar as Zoe sat down. She watched him for a moment as her key pulsed faintly in her pocket, willing it to notice his, to choose him. After everything she'd been through, she was ready for her love story.

As Cailean stepped up to the bar, the barkeep approached him immediately, a fae male with chestnut hair and dark brown eyes. While fae did not age like humans, Zoe assumed he was close to Cailean's father's age. After a few moments of chatting, the older male nodded to Cailean, sliding a room key across the bar before walking into the kitchen.

Cailean returned to the table a moment later, the barkeep following with a tray in his hands. Moving aside, he allowed the older male to place the tray on their table before taking a seat across from her.

"I figured you would want to eat before going upstairs."

The plate of grilled meat and eggs in the center of the table made Zoe's mouth water. Since escaping Lord Argall's camp, they hadn't had much time to rest, so they hadn't eaten anything substantial for a while.

With a nod, she pulled a plate of food and mug of tea closer to her. "I would. Thank you for everything."

"You're welcome, sunshine, but you don't have to thank me for taking care of you."

Although they had escaped the Court of Knowledge and were relatively safe, Cailean's face was still tinged with tension. The dark shadows surrounding his equally dark eyes revealed his exhaustion. As he bit into his breakfast, his movements were slow, as if he needed sleep more than food. She didn't need to ask what was troubling him. Even though they were safe, the others were still out there, and nothing was certain about their safety, as well as her mate's.

"What did the barkeep say?" Zoe asked, growing increasingly uncomfortable with the silence that went on for several minutes while they ate.

As Cailean chewed his food, he set his fork down on his plate. "It appears that Edric knows Blaze well. If they arrive while we sleep, he'll send someone up to the room to wake us. Aside from that, all we can do is wait."

After finishing their breakfast, Zoe and Cailean headed up the stairs to their room. Zoe's stomach flipped at the thought of staying in a room alone with Cailean, partly out of desire and partly out of anxiety. She'd had plenty of sex, but none with a male whose mere touch sent a jolt of electricity through her body. It didn't matter if her mate was looking for her or not, she wanted Cailean. She wanted him badly.

It was quiet in the hall of the inn on the second floor, with most rooms either empty or their residents sleeping. They moved down the lantern-lit corridor in silence, Cailean leading Zoe while holding their supplies, which weren't many. In the chaos of her capture, Elianna managed to keep possession of her bag. Without it, she would've had no extra clothing or toiletries.

When they got to one of the doors halfway down the hall, Cailean pulled the key out of his pocket and unlocked it, opening the door for Zoe to enter ahead of him.

It was a small room, with only one bed and a small table against the wall, but it would be enough for their needs. One bed would only serve to make things more interesting, which Zoe wasn't against. She wanted to sleep in the same bed with Cailean. She longed for the comfort and protection he offered, and to explore why her body was so reactive to his. With any luck, their friends would arrive later that day, and they would be able to set off for Blaze's property by morning. Once that happened, they would no longer be alone.

The room smelled of old wood and musty air, but it was surprisingly clean. Sunlight streamed in from two windows on one of the walls, but there were candles set throughout in case they needed more light. Although Lord Argall's manor had electricity, the rural tavern did not. Zoe stepped into the room, peeking into the door along the side wall and exhaling a sigh of relief when she saw a bathtub against the wall. After days on the run, living in tents and a dilapidated old cabin, she felt dirty and realized she probably smelled as foul as she felt.

"I don't have any clean clothes, but I need a bath, so I hope you won't mind that I sleep naked."

With a sense of safety, Zoe's usual snarky personality resurfaced. Cailean's eyebrows lifted nearly into his dark hairline as his eyes grew wide. It appeared that he was surprised by her comment, and she loved that. She had no qualms about making the first move if she needed to.

A moment of awkward silence passed before she turned on the tap and began unlacing her tunic. Cailean cleared his throat.

"No—I—um—whatever makes you comfortable, but Edric did say he would send clothing for you up to the room a bit later. I can go back and check with him."

Seeing how he shifted on his feet and stared at the floor as he spoke made Zoe grin. Her companion was certainly more reserved than she was, and she intended to change that. After turning her eyes to meet his, her tunic fell to the ground, exposing her bare breasts. "Do you have any other clothes we can change into? I could always wear one of your tunics."

As she stood half naked in front of him, Cailean's lips parted and he scratched the stubble on his chin before looking away. When he met her gaze again, his cheeks were flushed.

"Edric is bringing clothes for me as well. I don't have to sleep naked though. I can just put my—"

She cut him off, amused at how he stumbled over his words. "No. You are not climbing into a clean bed with dirty clothes. That's not going to happen."

Chapter 3

Cailean

The sight of Zoe standing nearly naked in front of him forced every thought from Cailean's mind, but his cock definitely had plans for her body. While he debated what to do next, his heart pounded as he looked anywhere but at her. He craved her, his mouth watering with the need to kiss her, but she wasn't his.

There was a part of him that wanted to go downstairs and rent another room, so they didn't have to sleep together. The temptation would be too great if they did. There was nothing more he wanted than to bed her, but he wanted more than that- he wanted her to be his mate. The idea that her mate was searching for her filled him with hesitation. Despite this, the other part of him, the part that thought with his heart, told him that even if he had only one night with her, he needed to touch her. It didn't matter if his key didn't know she was his, he knew.

Looking at her again, as her blond hair hung in waves over her full breasts and her porcelain skin looked too soft to not touch, he made up his mind. Crossing the space between them at nearly a jog, he pulled her into his arms, pressing his lips to hers.

There had always been something special about their touch, a surge of power that made them want to touch again. However, the moment her lips met his, it felt like destiny.

Closing his eyes, Cailean groaned, sliding his hands into her hair and pulling her head back so he could kiss her deeper. Zoe's full lips were pillow soft, her tongue slipping between his as her hands slid in between them, pulling at the laces of his tunic. His hands roamed over her body, exploring the curves of her waist, the dip of her spine, the swell of her hips. His heart raced as his body responded, fire flooding his veins, making his head spin as his cock throbbed in his trousers. The only thing he wanted was to be lost in her.

Cailean lifted her, her legs wrapping around his waist as he carried her out of the bathing room and to bed. After lying her gently on the bed, Cailean pulled his tunic over his head and crawled over her, melting into her kiss again. She shivered beneath him, her bare skin like warm silk against his chest as her hands slid up his back.

Despite his desire to keep touching her, to do everything with her, he pulled away, his conscience giving him pause.

"Are you sure you want to do this? We don't have to do this, Zoe. I—"

She slid her fingers into his hair, pulling him back against her lips in a punishing kiss, putting an end to his rambling. He groaned into her mouth, his tongue stroking hers to taste her. Although he knew he should, it was impossible for him to deny her.

His lips left her mouth, and he traced his tongue up her neck column, kissing, licking, and sucking her sweet skin. Head tilting back, her back arched against him. Every soft sigh she made, every gasp, drove him to kiss her body more. There was nowhere on her he didn't want to taste.

Pulling away for a moment, he trailed a finger down Zoe's cheek as he took in her beautiful face. She'd been through so much in her life before and after entering his world. The only thing he wanted to do was make her happy, but there could be undeniable consequences if they moved further.

"We shouldn't do this, Zoe. I'm not your mate."

It wasn't that he didn't desire her. While he didn't want the moment to pass him by, the idea of turning her over to another crushed him. There was no way he could handle that, especially not after being inside her. If the shoe were on the other foot, he would want whoever had his mate under him to refuse.

He knew there was nothing he could do. Even though his heart would break, he knew he had to let her go. If they became closer, he would experience indescribable pain if he saw her with another male, and he wanted to spare her that same pain.

Making a sound of annoyance, Zoe dug her nails into the muscle of his back, his eyes falling shut with her touch.

"Stop thinking about my damn mate, Cailean. I'm tired of thinking about some stranger who may or may not show up. So much of my life has been out of my control- my cancer, my abduction, my slavery..." She hesitated, her eyes turning glassy. As he wrapped his arms around her, his heart split in two. "I'm tired of it. I just want to make my own damn decisions."

Cailean nodded and kissed her cheek before looking into her eyes. "And what do you want, Zoe? The only thing I want is for you to have whatever makes you happy." Despite worrying that her mate might turn up, he meant it. In the end, she deserved happiness.

The side of Zoe's mouth lifted with a sad smile as a tear slid down her cheek. "You are the one I want. I know we just met, but I know there's something between us. Tell me you feel the same way."

Words could not adequately describe how much he wanted her, or how deeply he felt for her, how much she made his pulse race.

Instead of using words, he slid his hand around the back of her neck, pulling her into a kiss.

When they touched this time, there were no reservations. He groaned as his hand trailed down her chest, cupping the supple skin of her flawless breast. His fingers teased the stiff peak before he lowered his head to kiss it, savoring the way her nipple felt on his tongue.

"Are you saying you want this too?" she panted, lust and doubt warring in her tone. "Do you feel what I feel?"

As Cailean pulled his lips away, he gazed into her blazing blue eyes once again. "When we touch, electricity warms me from within, an undeniable sense that we belong together, even if my key remains silent. I could be wrong, but I don't believe I am." He paused, leaning over to kiss her lips. His fingertips gently trailed along her face, brushing away the hair that had fallen across her forehead. As she lay beneath him, her heart pounded in perfect harmony with his own.

"Yes, Zoe, I feel what you feel. I want you more than life. I love you more than I love myself. If you want to ignore our keys—if you wish to melt them down and make them into wedding bands—I would do that if it allowed me to be with you."

Sliding her fingers into his hair, Zoe pulled his mouth to hers. The ferocity of her kiss left him breathless. His grip tightened on her, his heart swelling with love. At that moment, he knew he would do anything to be with her. This amazing female wanted to be with him after years of suffering and loneliness. Knowing this, he intended to move mountains if it meant she would be his.

Zoe pulled him fully on top of her, the heat from between her thighs forcing a groan from him as his cock aligned with her center. Body throbbing with the need to be inside her, he pressed himself against her and her legs opened wider to give him access. They still wore their trousers, the thin layer of fabric the only thing preventing them from coming together.

Reaching between them, Zoe snaked her hand between his stomach and the waistline of his trousers, gripping his cock as her tongue slid against his. He groaned, leaning back on his knees and fumbling with the clasp on his pants. The way she bit her lip, squirming as she slid her own trousers down her porcelain thighs, only made his task more urgent. He'd intended to explore every inch of her, to learn every touch that brought her pleasure, but Zoe seemed to be impatient.

"Do you need help with those?" she asked, sliding her legs free before reaching for his hands. She batted them away and unclasped his buttons in mere seconds. Their eyes locked as she slid his trousers down his hips, freeing his aching cock from its prison.

Zoe grinned, a seductive look he knew other males had probably seen before and it sent fire through the possessive part of him. Crawling back over her, he intended to kill any male who tried to touch her again.

The fullness of her lips crushed against his, pulling him from his own thoughts. His body ached for her, his cock twitching against her wetness. Just a slight movement and he would have been inside her.

"I can't wait any longer, Cailean. Please stop hesitating."

His nostrils flared, her words catching him by surprise. It wasn't a hesitation, and he didn't want her to perceive it as such. Without another breath, he reached his hand between them, pressing his lips to hers as he slid inside.

Chapter 4

Zoe

The feeling of Cailean inside her was like fire in Zoe's veins. As her legs tightened around him, she breathed out a gasp. She needed him closer, deeper. Heat rushed through her as her fingers wrapped around his back.

"You feel so..."

Cailean's words trailed off as a deep groan rumbled out of him. With his lips pressed to hers, he sank in deeper, his cock filling her completely. She lifted her hips, submitting to him as his tongue sought hers. Their breaths intertwined as they moved together.

"Feel so what?"

The words were no more than breath as she spoke against his neck before sucking his salty skin hard enough to leave a mark. His body tensed beneath her as nails dug into the muscles of his back.

"Feel fucking perfect. You are perfect."

Zoe wanted to laugh, knowing she was far from perfect, but Cailean kissed her hard as he surged into her, taking any response she had and turning it into a moan.

His hand gripped her hip as their bodies moved together, his cock hitting the sensitive spot inside her and edging her toward her climax. She'd never gotten so close so fast, but when her orgasm hit her, her body bucked off the bed, her pussy tightening around him as waves of ecstasy surged through her body.

The sounds she made seemed to fuel his movements and he redoubled his efforts, thrusting deeper as his hands caressed her body, her breasts, working her until she was breathless. His desire and passion for her was evident in every stroke, as if he was determined to show her just how much he needed her. At that moment, when he was deep inside her and his climax had him groaning into her mouth and filling her with his seed, there was nowhere else in the world she would have rather been. He was hers and she was his, no matter what their keys said.

When Zoe awoke after falling asleep in post-orgasm bliss, Cailean still slept peacefully beside her with his arm draped over her waist. She watched him for a moment, taking in every feature of his handsome face, unable to stop a grin from lifting the corners of her mouth. Having worked in a brothel for a year, she'd had a lot of sex, but this was different. There was something special between her and Cailean.

Leaning forward, she smoothed his dark hair from his face and kissed him. He didn't wake, but he stirred, his arm wrapping tighter around her middle as he mumbled something she couldn't decipher.

Zoe slipped below the covers where Cailean was still naked, admiring his phenomenal body. He was sculpted like someone who'd been fighting with a sword his entire life. She kissed her way down his muscled stomach, making her way to the impressive cock that was already stiff and waiting for her.

Waking from her touch, he slid his fingers into her hair and groaned as she took his length into her mouth.

"Damn, Zoe." Pleasure laced his words, his voice deep and breathy. "I need you *now*."

She grinned against his sensitive flesh, tracing her tongue up the underside of his cock before taking him into her mouth again and sucking him deep.

Working him with her mouth and hand, she moaned as the salty taste of his precum hit her tongue. His body moved beneath her, his fingers tightening in her hair only encouraging her. She moved faster, her hand gripping his shaft as the head of his cock hit the back of her throat.

As she used her other hand to caress his balls, Cailean's hips bucked off the bed. With her name on his lips, his climax rocked through him and the salty warmth of his release filled her mouth. She swallowed it down, stroking him until he was spent and panting. As she licked his cum off her lips, he pulled her on top of him, pressing his lips against hers as he pushed his still hard length inside her.

After making love again, Zoe was ravenous. They dressed in the clean clothes Edric had left outside their room and went downstairs. The long ivory tunic and trousers Zoe had been given were too big, but she was just glad to have something to wear that didn't smell like sweat and dirt.

Unlike earlier that morning, when there had been few patrons in the tavern, many more fae sat on the barstools and at the tables, enjoying drinks and dinner. A male sat in the corner of the room, playing a cheerful tune on a stringed instrument Zoe didn't recognize from the human world.

Taking two stools at the bar, she scanned the room for her friends, her heart falling when she didn't see them.

Cailean got the barkeep's attention, ordering two mugs of ale and two plates of stew. It only took a few minutes for the meal to be placed in front of them, but Zoe's appetite had vanished with the worry that took its place. She still nibbled at her food, knowing she needed to eat, but every swallow took effort.

While seated on the bar stool next to Cailean, she watched the tavern door, hoping her friends and Cailean's family would come in with them. Only once she knew they were safe would her lungs stop seizing up in her chest. Elianna had risked everything to escape Lord Argall's manor and had insisted Zoe join her. She'd saved her when she didn't have to. After what they had endured to escape captivity together, they both deserved their happily ever after. If Elianna had died trying to rescue her from Lord Argall's men a second time, Zoe knew she would never forgive herself.

Hours had passed with no sign of them. The single male playing music was replaced by a three-piece band, their songs more excited than what preceded them. Cailean's arm wrapped around her waist, holding her close as they sipped on their drinks.

Even with Cailean's arm around her, and the love she felt for him in her heart, there were still moments when questions entered Zoe's mind, questions as to whether she would fall in love with the male who held her key's twin from the moment she met him. She couldn't imagine loving another male more than Cailean, but how the key worked was a mystery to her. The thoughts sickened her, tightening her chest and churning her stomach. Just the thought of falling for another filled her with guilt. She pushed away the thoughts, instead focusing on the love she shared with Cailean and the path they had chosen together. She knew that no matter what happened, she would always love him, and that was enough for her. As the shame in her chest threatened to consume her, and her hope of seeing her friends again drained with each sip of her whiskey, the bell above the door rang, drawing her attention.

As Elianna, Blaze, Fionn, and Baltair entered the tavern, relief struck Zoe in the chest, instantly releasing the tension that had kept her muscles tight. Overwhelmed with emotion, she fell to the ground, covering her face with her hands. Elianna crossed the room quickly, kneeling beside her and wrapping her in an embrace. As she looked over her friend's shoulder, Zoe watched Cailean join his father, brother, and Blaze at the bar, giving her and Elianna a moment together.

"When I was taken, I thought I'd never see you again," Zoe said, her voice shaking as she lifted a tear-stained face to look into her friend's eyes.

"But I'm here. We both are, and we're going to be okay."

As she glanced up at the bar patrons who had all stopped their conversations to watch the reunion, Zoe nodded, but the tears continued to fall. She blew out a breath and stood next to Elianna, their hands interlocked. "So, we're really free?"

Elianna squeezed Zoe's hand. "We're free."

Chapter 5

Cailean

After their long day's journey and battling Lord Argall's guards to save Zoe, Cailean's father, Baltair, and older brother, Fionn, retired to their rooms after eating their bowls of stew and having a few drinks. Having experienced the same ordeal, Blaze and Elianna followed shortly thereafter, leaving Zoe and Cailean alone once again.

Remaining at the table in the corner of the tavern, they sipped on mugs of whiskey. There was silence between them as their emotions settled from the highs and lows of the past few days. Zoe's key flickered, indicating her mate was getting closer, but she put it back in her pocket once Elianna left to go upstairs.

Even though tension was clearly visible on her face, Cailean knew she was actively trying to push it away. He wished he could relieve her of the burden, but it was up to her to decide what she would do next. When upstairs in their room, she'd all but declared she wanted to be with him and not with the mate who was looking for her. However, the key still remained in her pocket. Its presence was a constant reminder to Cailean that her mate was still in play, and that fact made it difficult for him to breathe. Still, as long as she allowed him to be close to her, he would be. It was important for him to let her make her own decisions, even if they weren't the decisions he wished she would make. Even if she ultimately chose her mate, he would support her in whatever decisions she made. He would accept her choice and try to move on, but he would always love her.

Because they hadn't yet discussed how they would share their blossoming relationship with the others, Cailean waited until Zoe was alone before wrapping his arm around her. She smiled and leaned into his embrace, the touch filling his chest with joy. The gravity of what they'd done hadn't completely sunk in yet, but the affection he felt for her was real. After finally touching all of her, he was having a difficult time keeping his hands to himself, even when the others were near. They both knew it was only a matter of time before their secret was out, but for now, they seemed content to keep it to themselves.

"How are you feeling?" he asked, running his fingers up her arm as he held her close.

Putting her cheek against his chest, she shrugged. "I'm just relieved everyone made it back safely. I was so worried."

He nodded as he sipped his remaining drink. "We'll have a lot to discuss and plan in the coming days, including what you'll do when your mate finds us. Unless you leave your key behind, he will find you, eventually."

The words were like acid on his tongue as he spoke them, and they created unmistakable tension in Zoe's body, but he needed to say them. He squeezed her harder, knowing he wouldn't be able to let her go, but he understood he didn't have a choice. He also knew that time was of the essence. Therefore, he was trying to make the most of the time they had together, but they needed to have a plan in place.

"I don't need to plan for a scenario where I leave with my mate. Cailean...I..." She shook her head slowly and looked away for a moment as though she needed to gather her strength to continue. "Cailean, there's no way, no scenario, where I will be leaving with anyone but you. I hope that's what you want because that's what I want." She looked back at his face, her eyes intense and sincere. "I *will* stay with you, whatever happens."

Relief flooded his chest as her sweet words met his ears, but he knew he needed to be cautiously optimistic.

Leaning his forehead against hers, he looked into her big blue eyes. "I want that too," he said, his voice full of emotion. He pulled her into an embrace, closing his eyes as a wave of love and contentment washed over him. He wanted the same thing, but no matter how much they talked about it, it wasn't that simple. It was possible that the magic in the key in her pocket would make her love her mate the moment she laid eyes on him. Even though the mere thought threatened to break him, Cailean couldn't pretend it wasn't possible.

As soon as they returned to their room, Cailean and Zoe fell into each other's arms once again, making love for hours. Despite the possibility that he might lose her to another, he couldn't deny her or himself. Part of him believed that this would be the last time they would be together. When the night was over, and her mate found them during their travels, he knew his heart would be broken.

As they laid in each other's arms, he hugged her tightly, wanting to remember the feel of her body next to his for the rest of his life. Having lived without a mate for his entire life, Zoe was like the sun on a cloudy day. His greatest desire was to have her in his life. The worry remained, however, no matter how many times she told him she only wanted him.

When Zoe fell asleep that night, cuddled up against his chest, he watched her sleep for a long time, wishing he could keep her with him forever. But the fear of losing her always lingered at the back of his mind. He knew that all he could do was treasure every moment he had with her, and hope when he returned home, that she would be by his side.

It had been agreed that the group would meet at first light, wanting to waste no time before continuing their journey. With that plan in mind, after waking up the following morning, Cailean and Zoe quickly dressed, gathering their belongings and heading to the tavern.

With everything they'd been through, the group was ready to settle down in safety on Blaze's property. At least until Cailean, his father, and brother had to return home to the Court of Courage. Although he missed his mother, niece, and nephew, the idea of returning home weighed on Cailean's shoulders. Even if Zoe did remain with him, he realized she would be hesitant to leave her only friend. It was something they would need to discuss, but he wasn't against remaining near Blaze and Elianna until Zoe was ready to leave.

Since Blaze's home was only a few hours' ride from the tavern, the last leg of their trip was less hurried than the journey from the Court of Knowledge capital to the inn had been. They also knew Lord Argall's guards would not be able to capture them in the Court of Harmony because of the strict laws against stealing human women from another court. As a high-ranking aristocrat, Lord Argall would have been foolish to do so without the support of his own king. The lord who'd stolen them may have been powerful, but he was not foolish.

Even though she was no longer worried about being recaptured, Zoe's stomach still twisted with unease as the key vibrated in the pocket of her cloak. It reminded her that her mate was getting closer. She knew what she wanted. She wanted Cailean, but she wasn't looking forward to having to turn down the male who thought she would be his soulmate. The last thing she wanted to do was break someone's heart. Although she tried to ignore her key, pretending it wasn't signaling her, she knew it was only wishful thinking. He would find her, and when he did, she would have to face him.

Nestled between Cailean's thighs on Wallflower's saddle, his arm wrapped tightly around her waist as they moved at a leisurely pace. They hadn't yet admitted to their growing romance, but they weren't hiding it either.

As the group moved down the dirt roads, Blaze and Elianna kept to the front of their caravan, and Fionn held up the back, allowing Zoe, Cailean, and Baltair to travel safely in the center. The forest faded in the background, the trees thinning as the forest was replaced by fields of crops and wildflowers. Lifting her face to the sky, Zoe enjoyed the sun on her face as she inhaled the scent of the wildflowers and fresh air.

After spending so much time at Lord Argall's brothel, and the rest of her time in his manor, she'd always looked forward to having to work in his gardens. Just the chance to be outside had always filled her with joy. Now that she was free, she hoped to spend time every day out in nature, tending to the garden or learning to hunt with Cailean. These thoughts brought a smile to her face and she twisted her head so Cailean could hear her. "Do you think, one day when things settle down, that you could show me the sea? Bring me to the beach?"

He leaned forward, kissing her on the cheek. "I will bring you anywhere you want to go. As long as it's possible, then it can be our adventure."

Letting her body fall back against him, Zoe's eyes closed as she imagined all the adventures they could go on together. She could almost feel the sand between her toes and hear the waves crashing against the shore.

"I've never been to the sea, or at least I don't remember," she said, his chin resting on her shoulder so he could hear her. "I got sick when I was young, and we didn't live near the coast. The sicker I got, the more impossible it became to travel very far."

The loss of so much of her life, the loss of her childhood, was a pain she'd pushed far into the back of her heart, and even further into the back of her mind. It was a rabbit hole she wasn't ready to spiral into, so she changed the subject. "Are the coasts far from here?"

Cailean smoothed her hair away from her face with his hand, his calluses sending a shiver through her body when they ran across her cheek. "The continent is surrounded by the sea. If you return to the Court of Courage with me, the sea is not far from my home. We could ride down there and spend some time, rent a cottage right on the beach, make love right in the sand. It would be beautiful to see the water reflected in your eyes, to see the sunlight shine off your hair."

As Cailean nuzzled into Zoe's neck and she imagined the wonderful vacation he offered her, the pulsing coming from her pocket became frantic against her leg, drawing her attention. Unable to ignore it, she slid the enchanted object from her pocket, her heart sinking into her stomach. Her face twisted with dread as it turned into a solid light in her hand, dropping it as if it had burned her.

Cailean stiffened behind her, pulling on the reins. Once the horse stopped, he dismounted and picked up the still glowing key. His face was stoic, but she felt the pain radiating off him. It was the same pain churning inside her.

"Don't."

Pressure built in Zoe's chest, her control over her nerves waning. She didn't want the key. She didn't want the key to bind her to a man she didn't want to be with. Her soulmate would not be chosen by a key, not after suffering through all that she'd been through in the brothel and in her life before. It would be her choice. The key had clearly been right about Blaze and Elianna. However, if the key in Cailean's hand was hers, and not someone else's that Pith grabbed by accident, then it was wrong about who she should be with. She needed to get as far away from it as she could before her mate found her.

The rest of the group stood back, remaining quiet to allow Cailean and Zoe their privacy. However, after a few moments, Eliana dismounted her horse and darted to where Zoe was still sitting on her mount and staring at the key in Cailean's hand.

"Zoe?" Cailean took a step toward her, the key in his hand like an ember threatening to burn out, but she shook her head.

"No, Cailean. I don't want it. Leave it here. We can move on. Just leave it."

Not seeming to know what to do, Cailean stood before the woman he loved, holding the key connecting her to another male, but he didn't drop it. Zoe's heart beat erratically, her lungs not seeming to take in enough air as she watched him.

After a few moments, Blaze led his horse closer to where they gathered, his voice low as he said, "We can't keep standing here. Someone is coming, and I think we all know who it is. Whether you want to take the key or leave it, Zoe, you need to decide now."

A crumpled expression appeared on Zoe's face as her eyes stared up at Blaze's. "I know I'm supposed to feel it when he's near, but I have no feelings for him.

The key senses him, but my body doesn't. Shouldn't that tell me something? Shouldn't that tell me that he's not mine?"

"Maybe it isn't like that for everyone," Elianna replied, her statement more of a question. "Maybe it's worth meeting him, just to know for sure."

When Cailean moved closer, his steps were hesitant, but the key in his hand remained solid as he held it up to her. Her attention was drawn to it, but she did not take it. "If you don't want to leave with your mate, you don't have to. We won't let him take you. But, Zoe, please don't leave this day with regret, no matter who you choose."

Numbness spread across her body, every ounce of her exhausted and empty. Holding out her hand, she allowed Cailean to place the key between her fingers before falling into his arms.

Seeing that the pair needed some time alone, the rest of the group walked away and waited in the shade of an enormous oak by the road, letting the horses graze.

Zoe stood in Cailean's arms, her cheek against his chest as tears soaked into the fabric of his tunic. He rubbed her back as a figure atop a black stallion rounded the bend, the illuminated key hanging from the male's neck. Too heavy to beat, her heart dropped into her stomach. It was too late to run.

Dressed in a Court of Chaos uniform, the male that approached Zoe was handsome, but her heart did not leap for him. Her body did not call for him. She glanced toward her key, the golden metal pulsing and shining as it desperately tried to tell her the male in front of her was hers, but all she could say was "No."

The soldier stared at her incredulously, his own key reacting the same way. "No?"

While she held out the key to the male who was supposed to be her mate, Cailean tried to intervene, but she didn't even acknowledge him. The Chaos soldier's green eyes were wide as he reached out to grab the key. Once the enchanted metal was no longer in her fingers, she turned her gaze toward Cailean, exhaling.

"I know this key is supposed to determine who I'll love and spend my life with." As she wiped a tear from her cheek, the intensity of her decision made it difficult for her to breathe as she returned her gaze to the Chaos soldier. "But it's wrong. I'm sorry. I'm sure you will make a fantastic mate for someone, but that person won't be me. Maybe when the other women are freed from Lord Argall, then you'll find what you're looking for."

No one spoke for a long time. Zoe turned back to Cailean when he reached for her hand, his dark eyes capturing her attention. "Zoe, you don't have to choose today." His jaw tensed as he squeezed her hand, his thumb caressing her fingers. "What if you needed some time with him, just to be sure?"

Before the words had even left his mouth, Cailean's face was filled with pain and Zoe's head was already shaking.

"I don't need time," she said without hesitation. "I've made up my mind."

The Chaos soldier turned the key over in his hand before looking back up at Zoe. "What women? Why does Lord Argall have them?"

Zoe was surprised that Niall, the male she had assumed was expected to be her mate, had not seemed angry with her for rejecting him after he finally found her. After interacting with him for a few minutes, it seemed that he understood why. She was relieved that he had been so understanding, and she felt a newfound respect for him as a result. Instead of being angry and bitter, he had remained calm and collected, respectful of her decision. As she had not felt any sparks when he was close to her, he probably noticed the same thing. Thus, she became even more certain of what she had suspected all along. Pith had given her the wrong key.

Since Zoe's key had been given to her by the curmudgeonly brownie at Lord Argall's manor, Zoe was convinced he had grabbed the wrong one. With the magic-blocking safe full of dozens of keys, Pith could have easily taken whatever key was the most sparkly. She didn't know how the magic worked, but it was unlikely he knew exactly which one was hers. They were in a hurry to escape that night. Since they were rushing to escape, they had no time or way to verify that the key he'd given her had actually belonged to her.

Moving forward, her only hope was to discuss the issue with Pith if she ever saw him again and encourage him to retrieve the correct key. It didn't matter to her, however. She would never allow an object to choose her life partner for her. Not anymore. What she was more concerned about was getting the incorrect key back to the woman who it belonged to so Niall could finally find his true mate. She didn't want Pith's error to cause one of her friends to miss out on their future happiness.

When they left the side of the road where Niall had found them, he asked if he could follow them to Blaze's property to talk more about the women being held by Lord Argall. Knowing his mate was probably still there, he wanted to be a part of the rescue effort. After fighting against the Court of Chaos years ago, however, Blaze probably found the idea uncomfortable. Nevertheless, Elianna's mate came to an understanding with Niall after speaking with him, allowing him to tag along. Zoe believed Blaze's reasoning for agreeing to the plan was crucial to the success of their future endeavors. They needed as many who could wield a weapon as they could get to fight against Lord Argall's forces. With an offer of Court of Chaos assistance in front of them, they could not refuse him.

As they continued their journey across the countryside towards Blaze's rural cottage, Zoe wondered who at the manor was Niall's mate. With all the women the lord had already sold off, there was a chance his mate had already been sent away, but she hoped that wasn't the case. Although she knew all the women, she couldn't decide which of them would be best for him. She didn't know him well enough to guess.

While thinking about her friends still locked away at the manor, thoughts of Rebecca haunted her mind. Her friend had come to Ecromos just like she had, for a cure and the chance at a future, and it had all been taken away from her before she'd ever had the chance to meet her fated mate.

Lord Argall sold many of the human women he stole from the portal, but others, like Zoe, were used in his brothels. When high-ranking visitors came to the manor, he would often bring girls in to entertain them during their stay. One of those diplomats had murdered her beautiful friend when she'd been sent to service him during his stay. Even though Zoe didn't know exactly what had happened in the male's chambers that caused her friend's death, she didn't care. After leaving her home for a cure to her terminal illness, being captured and forced into a brothel, her friend had been killed by some horny asshole who didn't value her. A precious life was tragically wasted. There were not nearly enough females for Ecromos' males to mate with. This was the reason they created the magical keys to find human mates, and yet one of them died so senselessly.

Not wanting to spiral into grief, Zoe pushed the thoughts away but tears still burned at the back of her eyes. It was impossible not to feel angry about Rebecca's death. She deserved better. The only way to prevent this tragedy from happening again was to find a way to rescue the other women as soon as they could.

Rather than thinking about Rebecca and Niall's mates, she thought about her true mate, and Cailean's. The mere idea of it sent pain shooting through her chest. Sitting between Cailean's thighs on the saddle, his arms wrapped tightly around her and his breath on the back of her neck, she refused to believe they were meant for anyone but each other.

As Elianna and Blaze rode the horse beside them, Zoe could see how perfectly the key worked when it was in the right hands. The way Blaze whispered into Elianna's ear, her giggling, the way they looked at each other, and their affection for one another, there was no doubt that they were soulmates. In Zoe's case, however, the key-love connection had not worked, but that was okay since she was in love just the same. She had no regrets about the decision she'd made.

By traveling through the lowlands on the court's perimeter, the group steered clear of the capital. The detour was a longer ride, but it avoided prying eyes in case anyone was looking for them. The fact that Lord Argall shouldn't send people into another court to find them didn't mean he wouldn't. Although it was unlikely, they still wanted to be on the safe side. Most aristocrats had deep pockets and far reaches. The group would have been naive to believe the lord didn't have friends or allies in his neighboring court. With that in mind, the group kept their eyes open for anyone who might be following them. With there being very few people traveling down the rural road, there had been no signs of pursuit.

Niall rode beside Blaze, conversing with him for most of the journey. Still wearing his crimson Court of Chaos uniform, he carried himself like a soldier, and had the body of one too. As far as Zoe could tell, he was a kind male who would be a good mate for any woman at the manor. He'd traveled a long way to find his mate, showing how desperately he wanted her, and the way he'd handled Zoe's rejection showed his patience and respect.

In an ideal world, she hoped Raven would be his true mate. Raven deserved happiness after everything she'd experienced at the manor, and after the beating she'd received just days before Zoe and Elianna escaped. Every woman on his property had their own story, however, and deserved happiness just as much. In a perfect world, every single key would be recovered from the safe in Lord Argall's office, and would be returned to the woman it belonged to so their mate would be able to find them at last.

It was late afternoon by the time they arrived at Blaze's farmhouse. Exactly as he described it, the cottage was surrounded by fields of crops in every direction, giving them the privacy they needed. In the distance, a forest stretched to the snow-capped mountains on two sides. As Zoe looked out over the fields, she heard birds singing in the trees and the soft rustle of wind in the trees. There was a sense of peace and tranquility about the location that she desperately needed. Tension continued to release from her body the further away they got from the lord's manor. She was finally starting to realize she was safe. It wasn't something she'd experienced since she was a child. There had always been one danger or another. With Cailean's skin against hers, surrounded by their friends, danger finally seemed far away, and she didn't know what to think about that.

Following the others, Cailean led their horse toward the awaiting stable with one arm wrapped protectively around Zoe's waist. Ever since they'd made love, he always seemed to need to touch her, and she loved it.

When they arrived at the wooden structure, Cailean dismounted and helped Zoe to the ground. No longer under the facade of being just friends, he held her close, leaning down to kiss her. The touch warmed Zoe's body, the rest of the world slipping away as she gave in to the need to be with him. The moment his lips left hers, it took her a moment to catch her breath. Gazing into her eyes, he tucked her hair behind her ear and traced his fingers along her cheek. Her eyes fell closed for a moment, savoring the love that blossomed in her chest from his touch.

"Do you regret your decision?" he asked, his gaze soft and searching. "Even a little bit?"

Zoe slid her arms around his waist and laid her head against his chest, listening to his strong heartbeat. "Not even a little."

Whether or not he believed her, she had no regrets. In his arms was where she was meant to be.

Her peripheral vision caught Niall dismounting from his horse and leading it back to the stable. No part of her wanted to let go of Cailean and run to the other male. It was Cailean who made her body sing, not Niall. Although her key did not recognize it, she knew it was true.

Cailean kissed her again, a languid touch that made her toes curl in her boots. His touch was a mixture of relief and desperation. It only made her more determined to show him how much she loved him. She wanted to eliminate any doubts he might still have.

"I'm glad," he said as he slid his hand up to cup her cheek. "Because I wasn't sure how I would let you go. I love you too much to see you with someone else, but I want you to be happy no matter what."

"Do you want me to take her?" Blaze asked, reaching for Wallflower's reins and interrupting their moment. "I will get her some water and hay. You two can get comfortable inside. At least for now, I have enough space for everyone."

With a genuine smile, Elianna and her mate walked away from them. Zoe couldn't help but watch them as they disappeared into the stable, in awe of how much they loved each other already. She'd been there from the moment they met, and it was like something was innate between them, creating a bond that some never experienced. After everything Elianna had been through, it was truly beautiful to see.

"Shall we?" Cailean asked, lifting their joined hands and drawing her attention back to him. As she nodded, she allowed her new mate to lead her to the safety of Blaze's home where she could finally relax, at least for a while.

Chapter 8

Cailean

Although Cailean had no idea what to expect in Blaze's home, he was pleasantly surprised by its cleanliness and size. For an unmated male, it seemed to have been built for a family. He was reminded that his own house would be too small if he and Zoe eventually had children, but it would suffice until then.

This cottage was constructed with large logs from the nearby forest, and the living room and kitchen were generously sized. There were also three bedrooms, each with its own bathing room. In spite of the fact that some of the spare bed chambers were not large, all of them had beds that could accommodate two people. The fact that Cailean would be able to lay in the comfort of a proper bed with Zoe made him very happy.

He didn't know how long they would stay with Blaze, but he didn't want to interfere with Blaze and Elianna's new relationship. Even so, he realized that Zoe would want to stay near her friend, at least for a while. Without any other family in Ecromos, they were as good as sisters. In order to build a life for herself in their world, she would need all the support she could get.

Upon entering one of the spare bedrooms, Cailean placed his bag on the bedside. He reached out to wrap Zoe in his arms, kissing her deeply. "Would you like a bath, or do you want to see what the others have planned?"

Nodding, she pulled away from his chest, her face bright with a sleepy smile. "I would love nothing more than a bath and a nap. My butt hurts from sitting on that horse for so long. It would be nice if we could get some rest before we go out to see the others."

Zoe's idea brought a smile to Cailean's face as well. It showed him that she wanted to spend time with him and was not concerned about the other male. If she was willing to get in bed with him, while the other male was in the same house, then she really had made up her mind. The relief that filled Cailean helped ease some of the tightness in his chest. He'd told her he was willing to let her leave for her own happiness. However, he would have been lying to himself if he didn't admit that he at least thought about stealing her away, if necessary, to keep her.

Giving her one more kiss on the lips, Cailean sauntered into the bathing room, turning on the tap to fill the tub. Zoe remained behind in the bed chamber for a short while, digging through the bag she'd gotten back from Elianna. "Eventually, I'm going to have to go shopping and get more clothes. All I have is what Pith grabbed for me in a rush, and it isn't much."

"I will bring you into town tomorrow or in the next few days, and get you whatever you need, unless you need more time to rest," Cailean said, sticking his head out the door.

After grabbing a tunic from the pile, she walked towards the bathing chamber, untying her tunic as she went. "We can definitely go tomorrow, if that's okay with everyone else. I just hope the town isn't too far away. It would be a shame to have to travel too far just yet after how far we've just traveled. If there's nothing nearby, Elianna and I will figure something out."

With the water near full in the bathtub, Zoe stepped in as the steam sent tendrils through the air. Once submerged, she reached for Cailean's hand, gently squeezing it. "Are you planning to join me, my mate?"

The question sent a shiver through Cailean. His nostrils flared and he let go of Zoe's hand to tug off his tunic and trousers, tossing them to the floor.

"If you don't mind me taking up the entire space," he responded, his tone playful. After slipping into the tub behind her, he pulled her between his legs.

Leaning her head back against his chest, Zoe sighed. He moved his hands to her shoulders and kneaded them to ease the tension.

At that moment, there was nowhere he would've rather been. Even though it wasn't their home, it was as close as they could get at that moment. As he sat with her, he wondered what their own home would be like, and if they would ever have a family. The fact that she called him her mate meant more to him than she realized.

"So, are you accepting me as your mate, without knowing what your key will choose for you?"

Turning to look up at him, she puckered her lips. He leaned in for a kiss, lingering for a moment as he trailed his hand up her stomach to her breast, caressing it gently. She let out a small moan as his fingers circled her nipple. A smile spread across his face as he gazed into her eyes.

"As I've said before, my mate, I'm not letting anyone or anything choose who I'm meant to spend the rest of my life with, except me. So, to answer your question, yes, I accept you as my mate. If the time ever comes when I get my correct key back, we can melt it down and make wedding bands out of it, just like you said before."

Chuckling, Cailean filled a glass with water and poured it over Zoe's body. When the warm water hit her skin, she groaned. Cailean watched as the droplets rolled down her breast and across her flat stomach before reuniting with the water below.

"You are incredibly sexy, my sunshine. If I didn't tell you that before, I wanted to make sure to tell you now."

Looking up at him again, Zoe ran her fingers down the stubble on his cheek. "You are too. Why do you think I'm in the tub with you right now?"

The mischievous look on her face told him she would have been in the tub with him even if he had an unfortunate appearance. Still, the compliment filled him with pride.

Sliding his hands to her breasts again, he gently pinched her nipple with his fingertips, enjoying how the sensitive flesh pebbled at his touch. With her head against his chest, Zoe closed her eyes and slid her hand between her thighs, rubbing between her folds as he touched her breasts. Cailean's cock stiffened, pressing uncomfortably against Zoe's back. Using his other hand, he traced circles around her navel before slipping it between her legs. As he brushed his fingers against her soft folds, she gasped.

"Come," he whispered into her ear. "Sit on my cock, sunshine. I need you now."

With no hesitation, Zoe lifted onto her knees, her beautiful body dripping with water as she spun around to straddle him.

The first slide of his cock into her warm cunt pulled a groan from deep in Cailean's chest. Her lips slammed against his, stifling her moans as their bodies moved together. While he didn't know where the others were, he didn't doubt the others could hear their lovemaking if they were in the house.

Zoe rode his cock slowly, seating herself fully before sliding up again. The tight squeeze of her cunt made it almost impossible for Cailean not to climax as he rolled his hips to match her rhythm. Their kisses moved in time with their bodies, the languid dance of their tongues only heightening the experience.

Running his hands down her back until he caressed the curve of her backside, Cailean paid attention to every detail of her flawless body, wanting to memorize her completely.

In pursuit of her own pleasure, Zoe sped up her movements, Cailean lifting his hips to meet hers and making the friction more intense. She threw her head back in total abandon, her body trembling with pleasure. Cailean felt himself spiraling closer, pleasure radiating through him as they moved together. With one final thrust, they both found their release in a passionate explosion. She bit into his shoulder to suppress her screams as her orgasm hit her, her body trembling with pleasure. As her body clamped down on him, his release slickened her insides. With their bodies still joined and trembling with aftershocks, she collapsed against him.

Chapter 9

Zoe

Everyone must have had the same idea, because when Zoe and Cailean awoke from their much-needed nap, the sun was shining in through the window, but the house was quiet. Pulling on the cleanest pair of trousers she had, Zoe followed Cailean as he stepped out of the bedchamber and into the main hallway. Low voices met Zoe's ears before they'd even made it into the main room.

Elianna and Blaze sat at the kitchen table, a kettle between them. They sipped tea with their hands interlaced, talking in hushed voices. Although Zoe hated to disturb the moment, the wooden floors creaked, catching Blaze's attention. He smiled at them, waving them over.

"Did the two of you sleep?" Zoe asked as she stepped past Cailean to hug Elianna.

Her friend nodded against her shoulder. "We woke up not long ago, though I feel like I could sleep for a week. Would you like some tea?" she asked as she poured water into another mug, setting it in front of an empty chair. "Fionn is roasting meat. I know everyone is hungry."

Cailean chuckled, glancing out of the window where his brother's fire was blazing in the field. "Let me guess," he said, moving to open the door. "My stubborn brother hasn't taken a moment to rest."

Although Zoe hadn't had much chance to get to know Fionn, he seemed like a male who got things done. Out of everyone in their group, he was the only one mated to another fae. His son was ill, which was why the Oathorne father and his sons had taken the journey to the Court of Knowledge. They sought a tonic to heal the child. If it hadn't been for his sick child, she might have never met Cailean.

Blaze shook his head as he pushed away from the table and stood. "I'm hoping now that we're awake, he'll lay down to catch a few hours of sleep. He's been patrolling the perimeter, although we are safe here. Your father is asleep in the other spare room, but Niall and Fionn have set up tents in the field."

Kissing Elianna on the cheek, Blaze crossed the room, heading outside with Cailean. Zoe sat beside her friend, looking forward to a day of rest and recovery. There was so much they needed to do, but it would have to wait a day.

"So," Elianna said, turning to face Zoe with a spark in her eyes. "You and Cailean, huh? Have you truly decided to part with your key?"

Although Zoe had been expecting the question from her friend, she hadn't planned her response, nothing aside from what she'd told Cailean and Niall. "I have." Steadfast in her response, she nodded. "It's time for me to make decisions for myself. I can't explain it, but I'm in love with him, and he's in love with me. I know it's too soon but..." Her words trailed off as Elianna placed a hand on hers.

Elianna smiled. "That's all that matters then. If you two are happy, then I'm happy for you. You don't have to explain yourself to me, Zoe. I've known Blaze for just as long, and I feel the same way about him. I don't know what it is about these fae males, but they certainly know how to treat their women."

Unable to stop herself, Zoe snickered. "And, I don't know about you, but when they love you, the sex is top notch."

A laugh burst out of Elianna's mouth, sending tea splattering across the table. "Well, Blaze was my first, but I would have to agree with you on that. I can't imagine it being much better."

Zoe and Elianna finished their tea and followed their mates outside, where the aroma of roasted meat lured them to the fire. Fionn and Cailean were carving a wild pig while Blaze and Niall were setting up an outdoor eating area. After all their time in the wilderness, it seemed they enjoyed eating in front of a fire. Either that or Blaze was trying to keep the mess outside. As pleasant as the weather was, Zoe didn't mind.

Cailean grinned as they approached before turning his attention back to the knife he was holding and continuing to prepare the meal.

"Can we help with anything?" Zoe asked, stepping around her mate to help Blaze and Niall with the chairs.

Despite the warmth of the sun, a cool breeze blew, rustling the fruit trees on one side of the property.

Taking a deep breath, Zoe inhaled deeply, savoring the crisp scent.

Taking a moment to wipe sweat from his forehead, Blaze glanced back toward the house. Baltair emerged from the house through the back door, his silver hair damp from the bath.

"I was about to tell you to make sure the old man was still alive," Blaze teased, dipping his head in Cailean's father's direction, "But it looks like the scent of a hot meal lured him out."

As soon as everyone was outside, the Oathorne brothers served the food and the group sat around the fire to enjoy the meal. The discussion was light. No mention of attacking the Court of Knowledge was made.

Zoe sat next to Cailean, their thighs touching as they sipped on a fermented wine Blaze had been keeping for a special occasion. They drank late into the night, enjoying each other's company and the freedom to just be together.

When Cailean and Zoe climbed into bed that night, falling into each other's arms as a newly mated couple, hope and joy filled their hearts as they drifted off to sleep.

Over the course of four days and nights, the group rested and planned. With their recent escape from Lord Argall's manor and the Court of Knowledge, they couldn't barge right back in. Not if they didn't want to get caught. Fionn and Baltair had left two days after they'd arrived, since Fionn needed to get the tonic he'd found back home to cure his ill child. He intended to return to help them rescue the human women from the Lord's manor. Even if he could not return to the neighboring court because of his family's needs, he hoped to send others who could assist. Baltair, however, did not intend to return. The long trip had weakened him, and he needed time to recover in the safety of his home.

With a promise to return to those who were missing their mates as well, or at least those who were willing to aid in the cause, Niall left shortly after Fionn. There was no longer a question as to whether he was Zoe's mate, but he gave the key back to her before he left anyway. It was his hope that she would be able to help him find his true mate later, when he followed the siren's call of her key and returned to her.

Chapter 10

Cailean

"Pardon me."

Cailean felt a light tapping on the side of his nose even while he was sleeping. He swatted at it without thinking, pulling Zoe's body closer to him as she slept.

"Pardon me, Mister Lazy Bones. Pith has very important work to do."

The high-pitched voice broke through Cailean's dream. As he opened his eyes, he squinted at the sunrise coming through the window, when he noticed the figure of a brownie filling his vision.

"What the—"

His statement was cut short when the tiny creature grabbed the pillow out from under his head and smacked it with its bony hand, trying to fluff it.

"You must wake up, Mister Lazy Bones and Miss Zoe. Pith has to clean this filthy room."

She groaned and rolled over to face the intruder. "Pith, what in the hell are you doing here?"

Getting up from the bed, Cailean reached over and grabbed his trousers from the chair beside it.

"Pith is trying to clean, Miss Zoe, but you and Mister Lazy Bones are in the way."

With a huff, Zoe climbed out of the bed, pulling a tunic over her naked body. Before they could even get out of the way, Pith had already started fluffing the pillows and mumbling about how no one appreciated him.

"Is this the brownie who gave you the wrong key?"

As Zoe turned around to face the tiny creature, fire flared in her eyes. He was so buried in blankets; he didn't seem to notice.

"Yes! You and I need to talk about the key you gave me, Pith."

"No time. No time," he muttered as he fluffed the pillows again, his wrinkled face set with concentration. "Pith has no time to talk right now because Mister Lazy Bones and Miss Zoe wouldn't get out of the bed and they made Pith late for his chores and no one cares about Pith..."

A frustrated groan escaped Zoe's lips as she opened the door to leave, Cailean at her heels as she bounded out. As far as the brownie was concerned, it appeared that he had no interest in talking to anyone else, at least at that moment.

The sound of voices came to Cailean's ears as they approached the main living area of the house. Elianna and Blaze hovered near the stove as food sizzled.

"I see Pith woke you up too," Elianna said, her lips twisting into a smirk before she returned her attention to her task. "It appears we have a new housekeeper."

Zoe rolled her eyes and fell into a chair at the table. "I need to ask him about my key, but he's caught up in one of his poor-me-mumble-monologues right now."

Dropping into the chair beside Zoe, Cailean reached for the kettle and poured water into two mugs before dropping a tea bag into each. Cailean had met brownies before and they were all the same, insisting on cleaning but complaining the entire time. "Does he do that often? Mumble to himself?"

As Blaze divided the eggs and grilled meat into four plates, he chuckled. "He mumbles a lot, and he's an early-riser, so don't expect to get a lot of sleep if he wants to clean your room."

"Good thing I don't usually sleep late," Cailean responded. "And thank you both for cooking breakfast. I'm starving."

Taking a moment to glance over her shoulder, Zoe seemed to be considering heading back to the bedroom in order to speak with the brownie. After a moment, however, she turned around and ate a bite of her meal instead. "Do you think he's planning to stay here, or return to Lord Argall's manor?"

Taking a sip of tea, Elianna swallowed her food and shrugged. "The only thing he told me was to get out of bed so he could do his chores. That was about an hour ago. We have been in here ever since."

A pop and crash echoed from the hallway as they ate their food, putting aside their conversation about Pith. When Cailean turned around, the brownie stood at the entrance to the living area, a pile of illuminated keys at his feet.

"Pith!" Zoe jumped up from the table and ran across the room, kneeling in front of the pile of keys in front of the creature. "What did you do?"

A wide grin spread across the brownie's face as he twisted his hands around the hem of his tunic. "Pith brought Miss Zoe her key."

"You brought more than just my key, Pith."

After joining Zoe on the ground, Cailean passed his hand through the sparkling golden objects, each one glimmering in a different pattern. "You know what this means, right? With the magic of the keys no longer being blocked, the males on the other side of these keys know their mates are in Ecromos," he said as he fell back on his heels. "But they won't be rushing to the manor to look for their mates. They're going to come here looking for them."

Approaching from behind, Blaze and Elianna lowered to the ground beside them.

"There are at least fifty keys here," said Elianna as she picked up one to examine the intricate pattern on its handle. "Which means some of these must belong to women who have been sold off, right? Lord Argall didn't have this many women at his manor when I was there."

Taking a deep breath, Zoe shook her head and sat on her bottom, folding her legs in front of her. "No. He didn't."

"I guess we will have the males we need to rescue the women," Blaze said as he touched Elianna's shoulder. "Although I'm not sure how we'll find the females that he's already sold off."

For a moment, Cailean began to wonder if the mate who had been chosen for him by his key might be among those sold, or even those at Lord Argall's manor, but he pushed the idea aside. As long as he lived, Zoe would be his mate, now and forever. The fact remained, however, that if his mate was one of those females, he would need to rescue her. Though he could not be with her, she still deserved to be happy and to be with a male who would love her.

"How will Zoe know which one is hers?" Elianna asked her mate, which caused Zoe to stiffen.

Cailean's heart sank to the bottom of his stomach as he reached over to take her hand, interlacing his fingers with hers.

"It should know her touch. If she holds hers, she should know in her heart that it is hers. She should be able to feel the energy inside it, the pull of her mate," Blaze responded.

"My mate is here," Zoe said without hesitation as she rose from the floor, pulling Cailean behind her to sit on the sofa. "I don't want to touch any of them. Either way, I don't want to know. It won't change anything."

"But Pith brought Miss Zoe her key," a tiny voice said from the kitchen. In the shock of the brownie dropping dozens of enchanted keys on the floor, Cailean hadn't noticed Pith disappear.

"Thank you for bringing them, Pith. You're an awesome friend," Elianna said as she rose from the ground, patting the brownie on the head. A blush of pink swept across his cheeks as his olive eyes opened wide. "But, Pith, does Lord Argall know you took these?"

Upon hearing Elianna's words, the creature's face fell, and he shrank back, pulling his floppy hat over his eyes as he shook his head. "Master would be very angry with Pith so Pith can't go back there." His eyes lit up as if something had been switched on a moment later, and a grin spread across his face. "Pith will clean *this* house from now on."

s Elianna and Blaze sorted through the keys, Zoe and Cailean headed outside to check their traps and hunt. In addition, he intended to spend some time training her with his weapons. Zoe was eager to learn and Cailean was happy to teach her. In the aftermath of all the things she had been through, Zoe wanted to learn how to defend herself. Despite her cancer, she had never seen herself as a damsel in distress in the human world. However, that had changed completely in the world of the fae. After being abducted twice, she didn't want to go through it again. She realized, however, that they would eventually have to face males seeking mates after the events of the morning. Since the other women weren't there, they didn't know how fae males would react when they arrived at Blaze's property and didn't find the mates they sought.

There was no guarantee that the keys would only lure in trustworthy males.

To Zoe's relief, no strangers lingered nearby when they left Blaze's house and headed toward the forest. At least not those they could see, or at least not yet.

"So," Zoe said, squeezing Cailean's hand tightly. "What will we hunt for?"

He pulled her hand against his mouth and kissed her knuckles. Despite the events that had occurred that morning, he seemed to be in a cheerful mood. As she thought about it, she realized he was probably looking forward to going hunting. Among the males in their small group, he was the most skilled hunter. Zoe hadn't had many lovers before crossing into Ecromos, but her history with hunters was nonexistent. Modern conveniences in the human realm made hunting a less important skill. In the fae world, however, where grocery stores were not around every corner, having a mate who could provide food was a definite perk.

"We will probably be able to kill a deer, but we will have to make do with what we can get. Having extra meat to dry would be great if we can catch something big. We'll need to store food for winter."

Her eyes scanned the fields around them as she nodded. The fear of being taken again haunted her even with Cailean holding her hand. Still, she tried to shake it off, not wanting to ruin their day. Drawing a deep breath, she smiled and turned back to Cailean, resolute to enjoy the day they had together. "That makes sense."

The farther they got from the keys, the freer Zoe felt. Even though her mind and heart were already made up and she had no intention of choosing another male, she was still curious about who the enchanted object would have chosen for her. It wouldn't do any good for her to know, so she pushed that curious part of herself to the back of her mind.

"How long do you think we should wait until we return to rescue my friends? They probably increased the security of the Court of Knowledge after our escape, which would make returning even more dangerous."

Cailean gently squeezed her hand. "We will have to try eventually, even though I have the same fear. Our decision will have to be made once we find out how many males show up for their mates, as well as if Fionn is able to send anyone back from his trip home."

"Oh, and Niall. He should also be returning with help," Zoe added.

Cailean nodded as he leaned over to kiss her on the cheek. "Yes. That will definitely be helpful as well. The more people we have to build an army, the better off we will be. When Blaze rode into town a few days ago, he mentioned that he had sent a letter to the king of this court. Since he served under the king in the war, he is confident that the king will support our return to the Court of Knowledge to retrieve the enslaved women. He is only waiting for a response. As long as the king supports our cause, he should provide us with weapons, resources, and people to fight with us."

Though Zoe knew Blaze had been to town a few days earlier, she hadn't realized he was sending a message to the king. Even though they were staying at Blaze and Elianna's house, they hadn't spent much time with them. As both couples were newly mated, most of their recent time had been spent getting to know their partners.

The purpose of Blaze's trip into town, Zoe assumed, was to inquire about a house for her and Cailean to stay in for a while. Blaze and Elianna made an offer for them to stay with them as long as they needed, but Zoe and Cailean wanted to have their own space. Even if they eventually returned to Cailean's home court, they thought it was best to move out soon so

they could start their own lives together. From what
Zoe had heard, Blaze had a friend with a vacant cabin
in the woods close to town. Although Zoe enjoyed
being with her friends, she wanted to live somewhere
where she and Cailean could have their own privacy, a
place where they didn't have to worry about someone
hearing them through the walls. There was nothing
Blaze couldn't hear with his gifted hearing. With the
cottage in the forest, they would have the privacy they
needed while still being close enough to Elianna and
Blaze for dinners and visits when they wanted.

When Zoe and Cailean entered the forest, the
sun was already high in the sky, but the trees were
blocking it, leaving a large part of the trail in shadow.
As Cailean scanned the forest, their conversation
ceased in order not to scare away their prey. Zoe
took careful steps to avoid making noise as they both
moved along the path.

Seeming to hear something, he slipped the bow off
his shoulder, notched an arrow, and stared ahead. She
followed his line of sight, trying to see what had caught
his attention, but she didn't have fae senses, so nothing
stood out among the greenery and shadows. Holding
his fingers to his lips, he signaled for her to remain

silent. A moment later, his arrow flew, and a distant animal cried.

With a smile on his face, Cailean slung his bow over his shoulder, pulled his dagger from its sheath, and darted forward into the brush toward his prey. Because she didn't want to see Cailean putting the animal out of its misery, she did not go after him right away. She waited for a few moments, watching as Cailean's head of dark hair disappeared as he maneuvered through the brush.

Once he was nearly out of view, the hair on Zoe's arms rose and unease filled her. She tried to calm herself. She tried to convince herself that fear churned within her because she couldn't see her mate, but her instincts did not believe her. Her body told her something was wrong, but as she scanned the forest, nothing stood out in the darkness.

Afraid of being alone any longer, Zoe darted forward. The fear she felt was like a living thing, clawing at her insides, urging her to run. Before she was able to take no more than a few steps, a strong arm slipped around her waist, and another covered her mouth, holding her in place.

As she flailed her body to get free, desperation gripped her like an icy hand, blurring her vision. She tried to call out to Cailean, but all that came out was a muffled cry. Within moments, whoever held her lifted her off the ground and fled in a different direction, leaving her mate behind.

Chapter 12

Cailean

When Cailean returned to where he had left Zoe, the deer he'd killed in his arms, his mate wasn't there. She wasn't where he'd left her when he launched his arrow, at least. As he spun slowly in a circle, scanning the darkening forest for her, he wondered if she had just stepped off the path while she awaited him.

"Zoe?" His mind conjured up the darkest thoughts it could think of. The frantic beat of his heart caused him to feel dizzy and he dropped the animal in his arms. When the deer's body hit the ground, a resounding thump reverberated throughout the forest.

Cailean drew his sword from his belt and turned back toward where he had just come from, straining his eyes to see through the shadowy brush. "Zoe!"

A sinking sensation swept through his stomach, bile rushing up his throat. "Zoe!"

His breath was laced with guilt as he searched for her in the brush, hoping she hadn't fallen and gotten hurt, but she wasn't there. She was nowhere to be found. Almost as if she hadn't been there at all.

Leaving his kill to rot on the forest floor, Cailean fled from the forest and ran back toward the house. He searched the fields for Zoe's blond hair, calling her name repeatedly.

As he approached the house, the back door swung open. Blaze and Elianna moved toward him, most likely because Blaze had heard his panicked screams.

"What happened?" Elianna asked, her blue eyes wide as she scanned the land behind him. "Where's Zoe?"

Running right past his friends, Cailean headed toward the stables. "I searched everywhere I could think of where she could be. There is no way she would wander off by herself. She must have been taken!" he yelled over his shoulder. It was the only answer he could give. He had only left her side for a few minutes.

Although he didn't look back at them, he heard Blaze's heavy footsteps behind him. "Get inside and lock the door," Blaze told Elianna, but her resounding "No" came only a moment later.

"You should have learned the last time you told me to stay behind that I will never stay behind while everyone else fights. I'm going to search for my friend!"

Elianna's strength reminded Cailean of his own mate. Both females had endured more than anyone should have to. The two of them needed protection and to be able to live without fear. He ran faster, needing to get her back before she suffered more, but he had no way of knowing who had taken her or where they were headed.

Throwing the stable door open, Cailean slung the saddle onto Wallflower, strapping it in place. Blaze and Elianna entered a moment later, doing the same with his horse, Shadow.

"Any idea who could have taken her or where?" Cailean asked Blaze, since his friend was better acquainted with the area.

With a shake of his head, Blaze lifted Elianna up onto the saddle before climbing on himself. Cailean was already riding Wallflower back toward the forest before they left the stables.

"Unless we were followed, I don't think it could have been someone from the Court of Knowledge. All I can think of is it was someone who was drawn in by the keys," Blaze responded as they galloped across the field. "You go back to the forest. There are cabins and abandoned properties he could have taken her to. Elianna and I will head back toward the road, just in case he's taking her to town."

Putting his heels into Wallflower, Cailean urged the horse forward. Although he'd already searched the area near where he'd left her, he could cover more ground on Wallflower's back. It was likely that whoever had taken her was not traveling on foot, so he had to catch up with them. As he led his mount down the same trail, he and Zoe had taken upon entering the forest, he hoped he was going in the right direction. With no trace of her, there was no way to know. Taking a deep breath and gritting his teeth, Cailean focused on the task at hand. Zoe had to be found, and time was of the essence. He had to close the gap between them before it was too late.

When Zoe's abductor had gotten her far enough from Cailean to prevent him from hearing her, he stopped and lowered her to the ground. Then he wrapped something around her mouth. Whatever was on the gag knocked her unconscious within moments.

When she awoke again, groggy from the substance he had used on her, her vision was still too blurry for her to see anything. However, she knew from the floor beneath her and the stale, dusty air that she was no longer outside. She collapsed on the wooden floor, her heart wrenching in pain. Her breathing was labored as she yanked on the door handle, trying to make sense of the situation. She was trapped. A chill ran down her spine, dread racking her stomach.

"Cailean!"

It didn't matter how many times she shouted his name; she knew he couldn't hear her. The person who had stolen her would not have kept her close enough for him to find her. She sobbed as she swayed on her knees, letting herself fall over onto her side when she couldn't hold herself up any longer. Her head rested against the ground, her body feeling numb despite the pain that coursed through her.

"Why are you doing this? Bring me back to my mate!" she screamed, hoping her captor could hear her.

For a few long moments, the only noise that met Zoe's ears was crickets and animals that came out at night. She rubbed her eyes again, squinting against the darkness to scan the room, realizing it was as dark outside as it was inside. That meant she had been gone all day, maybe even more than one day, but she couldn't be sure how long she'd been out.

Gathering her strength, she rolled up onto her knees and tried to stand, but her legs were weak. They buckled under her weight, dropping her back to the ground.

"Help me! Please!" After a few more moments, heavy boots approached the other side of the door. She skittered back on the floor, crouching in the corner and trying to make herself invisible as the cabin door swung open.

With a torch in his hands, she could tell her captor was a fae male, but he appeared older than her mate. His hair was a light golden color like hers, but his eyes were dark.

"Screaming will not do you any good, sweetheart. There's no one around to hear you."

The words ripped her heart open. She fell forward on her hands and knees as tears dripped down her cheeks and sank into the wooden floor.

"Why are you doing this? Take me back to my mate or he'll kill you."

Her captor's cruel laugh turned her blood to ice as he took a few more steps into the room. As he walked toward her, he dropped a dish of food and a glass of water on the floor.

"He can't kill me if he can't find me, sweetheart. As far as what I want to do with you... ell, I would think you would've figured that out by now."

Zoe braced herself against the wall as she tried to stand again, forcing herself to be strong.

"If you're trying to get a mate, sweetheart," she snarled, "This is not the way to do it."

He laughed, not a chuckle like before, but a deep belly laugh that turned her stomach.

"I didn't take you because I wanted a mate, although I might not mind having a small piece for myself because you are a pretty little thing. I took you because I could negotiate a hefty price for you and for what you have below the waist. So, eat dinner and get lots of sleep. I need you to stay pretty when my buyer comes to see you."

Closing the space between them quicker than she'd expected, he grabbed her, pulling her into him and pressing his groin against her abdomen. She thrashed; her body too weak to fight as his erection jammed against her already churning stomach.

"Don't fight it, sweetheart. You know you want this."

His grip on her tightened as he slid one hand up her side to grab her breast, squeezing hard enough for it to hurt.

"Get the fuck off of me!" she screamed again, lifting her knee and striking him between his thighs.

With a grunt, he doubled over in pain, giving her only a moment to move out of his reach. He recovered quickly and stormed toward where she was standing, his hand striking her across the face with enough force to knock her to the ground.

Fire lanced Zoe's cheek, the skin beneath her hand hot from the assault. She clenched her teeth, holding back her cries and waiting for the next strike as he loomed over her. After a few frantic beats of her heart, he snarled and turned away, moving toward the door. As soon as the door slammed shut, leaving her alone in the darkness, Zoe doubled over and vomited.

Chapter 14

Blaze

Shadow galloped at a rapid pace as a search for Zoe sent Blaze and Elianna riding toward the nearest town. Blaze was enraged at the knowledge that someone would abduct another male's mate, especially so near his home. His heart raced as he feared for his mate. It was impossible for him to imagine what would have happened if Elianna had been abducted instead of Zoe as she hung laundry or tended the garden. To his relief, his mate was safe in his arms, but they needed to find Zoe before she could be harmed.

As Elianna and Blaze rode down the dirt path toward Mosshaven, they kept a watch out for Zoe or for the males summoned by the keys Pith had brought that morning. As they approached the nearest town, they had yet to encounter another soul on the road, which was not unusual in such a rural place, but he knew they were coming.

After arriving in town, Blaze attached Shadow to a tree outside the local tavern and took his mate by the hand. Having lived there for a long time, he knew many people, so there was a chance someone knew something. At mealtime, the tavern was the right place to find people he recognized. As they walked in, every eye in the tavern turned toward him and his human mate, and the conversation slowly died away. Blaze pulled Elianna closer, guiding her toward the bar.

Due to its rural location, the Gray Flame Tavern was a locals' hangout, so Blaze was surprised to find so many unfamiliar faces sitting at the bar. He had no doubt that some of them had arrived after being summoned by the keys that morning. Having held on to his own key for so long, he knew what it was like to hear the call of his mate's key. His front yard would be flooded with these males if they were looking for their mates, which filled him with a sense of dread. While they could provide extra swords for the rescue effort, he didn't like the idea of strangers around her. He knew what it was like to be drawn to his mate, but he did not know whether all the males who would appear on his property were virtuous. In light of what had happened to Zoe, he didn't want to put Elianna at risk.

As they approached the bar, Blaze pulled out a stool and sat beside her. The bar's owner placed two mugs of ale in front of them, raising an eyebrow at his old friend. Seeing Palos' questioning glance, Blaze realized it was due to the beautiful human woman seated next to him, but he did not have time to discuss his new mating. They needed to find Zoe.

A grin spread across Palos' face as he said, "I see you've made some changes in your life."

Sliding his arm around Elianna's waist, Blaze kissed her on the cheek. Elianna blushed, sending love radiating through Blaze's chest. She smiled at Palos, who gave her a friendly nod in response. "certainly have, but I am here for an even more urgent purpose. Is it possible to speak privately, old friend?"

After signaling for his wife to take over the serving of two males bowls of stew, Palos walked around the bar and waved Blaze over. Blaze helped Elianna off the stool, then led her into the bar owner's office before closing the door.

"Are you here to explain why I have so many new customers today?" he asked, sitting at the wooden desk.

Blaze nodded. "It's a long story, but let's just say that enchanted keys have found their way into my home today and are calling to males everywhere. This morning, my friend and his mate, who are staying with us right now, were hunting in the forest, and his mate was abducted. Although we don't know who took her or where she is, I have a feeling it has something to do with all the people who are undoubtedly headed toward my home."

For a moment, Palos regarded Blaze with a gray eyebrow raised. "I hear everything in this town, and it has been reported that a male has been asking around for his brother. As soon as the male's key began to shine this morning, his brother stole it. It appears that his brother is involved in the trade of human women."

Blaze pulled his mate close to him, caressing her arm as he felt a sinking feeling hit his stomach. "Where is the male looking for his brother? Could he still be here?"

Palos shook his head. "He was here just a few hours ago, but now he's gone. He lost sight of his brother in town after following him here. If he doesn't have his key, he might not be able to find your house, but if you search this area, you might find him."

Chapter 15

Blaze

"If you were summoned by a key," Blaze announced, the crowd of males turning their attention to him, leaving the room completely silent, "Then we need to go outside and talk."

Taking his mate by hand, Blaze dipped his chin at Palos before leaving. They walked out with purpose, the air of anticipation preceding them as their footsteps echoed in the silence.

Several males followed Blaze near the copse of trees where Shadow was grazing, waiting for him to continue. The men's faces were eager, ready to hear what Blaze had to say as the sun shone brightly above them. He waited several minutes to begin, however, making sure no one else would show up, so he wouldn't have to repeat his speech. Blaze wanted to make sure he had the full attention of all the men before he began speaking, so that his words would not be lost in the shuffle of people coming and going. Finally, with a deep breath and a confident voice, he began.

"There's a lot you should know about the keys and your mates, but I can't cover everything right now."

"Where are they?" demanded one of the males. The sentiment was echoed by others.

"There's an aristocrat in the Court of Knowledge holding them captive," Elianna interrupted, the strength in her voice filling Blaze with pride. In her short life, she had proven how fierce she was. Blaze felt his love for his mate continue to grow, admiring her courage and ambition that had made her such a force to reckon with.

One of the males with long, blond hair and sharp, green eyes stepped forward. He wore a tunic and trousers, brown leather boots, and a deep blue cloak. His body was adorned with numerous swords and daggers, showing how hard he planned to fight to protect his mate. He had a presence that commanded respect and attention, and the other males stepped back, allowing him to take the lead. "How do you know this?" he asked.

While Blaze was about to speak, Elianna stepped forward, commanding the crowd again. "I know this because I was there with them. My mate rescued me, but we couldn't save the other women in our hurried escape. We will need help to go back and free our friends, to free your mates. Argall has many guards, and possibly the support of his king, so we will need you to fight with us. My mate has sent a letter to the king and we are waiting for his reply, but we must all work together if we are going to rescue the other women and put an end to the flesh trade."

For a moment, the group conversed among themselves, the sound of their collective voices like a mumble Blaze could not make out. While they waited for the crowd to return their attention to them, Blaze embraced his mate, kissing her on the top of her head. There was almost a palpable silence when the males finally stopped talking. The entire group refocused on Elianna and Blaze, the air thick with anticipation as they awaited what the two would say next.

Elianna cleared her throat. "The lord took your mates' keys when he captured them from the portal. The magic in the lord's safe prevented them from summoning you until this morning when the keys were taken out of the safe. Since all the keys are in our home right now, we are not surprised that you are all here. There will likely be more on their way," Elianna continued, not waiting for their response. "But there's a more urgent problem right now. We know where most of your mates are, but my friend, Zoe, who escaped with me, was stolen again just this morning. We believe that someone came to my house after getting the signal from the keys and took her. Her mate is looking for her, but we are concerned about her well-being. According to what we've heard, the person who picked her up didn't want her as a mate and may even want to sell her. She needs to be found as soon as possible."

A male with short, black hair stepped forward, his dark eyes similar to Cailean's and Fionn's. "Why would we chase after your friend when our mates need us? Wouldn't it be better to rescue all the other females before something happens to them instead?"

As Blaze stepped forward to stand by Elianna's side, he took her by the hand. "We intend to return to the Court of Knowledge as soon as possible, but we can't do it without the king's support, and we can't do it today. It's only been a short time since we escaped. There will be tight security around the kingdom and the manor. There will also be people looking for us and expecting us to return, especially if they realize the keys are missing. In spite of our intentions, we cannot rush back without support and planning, or we will fail."

Outside the tavern, while the males talked among themselves and periodically asked Blaze and Elianna questions, another male approached from down the street, undoubtedly noticing all the commotion outside. The auburn-haired male looked intently at the group as if he belonged there. His broad shoulders and muscular frame gave the impression that he was an experienced warrior- someone who had seen his share of battles.

"Are you here because of the keys?" Blaze asked.

The newcomer nodded slowly as his eyes grew wide. "My key signaled to me this morning, but my brother took it. We weren't on good terms, and I don't know what he plans to do with it, but I have a bad feeling he intends to steal my mate and sell her, or use her for himself," he said, his voice cracking. The arrival of the male they were seeking, the one who could help them find Zoe, filled Blaze with relief. "Both of us have been waiting for a mate for a long time, although he is not deserving of one," the male continued. "When he realized what was happening today, my brother,

Jodoc, attacked me and took the key from me. After following him here, I lost track of him. I don't know where he or my mate are."

During the next several minutes, Elianna and Blaze explained everything to the male, who was named Mathias, and gained more information about his brother. After that, all the men in the group agreed to help find Zoe, so they could later join together with a larger group to rescue the women in the Court of Knowledge.

Following Blaze's instructions, the group dispersed in all directions in search of the kidnapped blond female. The group would reunite at Blaze's property by morning, earlier if they found her, and then make a plan to rescue the remaining women from the neighboring court. By then, they would hopefully have a response from the king.

Chapter 16

Zoe

After Zoe finished emptying her stomach on the cabin floor, she stood on shaky legs, moving to the door and pulling on the handle. While she wasn't surprised the door was locked, she tried again anyway, jiggling the handle to be sure. Her face was a mask of panic as she stepped away, defeat draining her energy. She had to find a way out, but the only windows in the structure didn't even look large enough to pass through. She was trapped. Taking a deep breath to steady her nerves, she looked around the cabin for any other sign of a possible escape route but saw none.

Fuck.

Although it was too dark outside the window to see if her captor was nearby, she still tried it, only to discover it was locked. She tugged at it again, hoping against all odds that it would somehow yield to her desperate tugging, but it didn't budge.

Her heart heavy with disappointment, she let out a deep sigh. After escaping Lord Argall's well-guarded manor, she should be able to escape the rickety cabin.

"I really need you right now, Pith," she whispered, scanning the open space for weapons. Aside from a bucket for her to pee in and a sink, there was nothing.

If it hadn't been for the resourceful brownie, she and Elianna might not have made it out of the lord's manor unscathed. While Blaze had been amazing, Pith brought Elianna's key to her in the first place. It was Pith who knew about the secret escape through the library. If she had a way to summon him, she knew he could break her out.

A pop sounded as she tried the other window across the room, followed by a whoosh of air. She turned, nearly falling to her knees, when the tiny humanoid creature stood before her, his floppy hat in his hands.

"Pith looked for Miss Zoe everywhere and could not find Miss Zoe, but when Miss Zoe said Pith's name..."

Closing the distance between them, she wrapped her arms around his miniature body, lifting him off the ground.

"I'm so glad to see you, Pith!" Her voice was a whispered sob as she dropped to kneel in front of him. He grunted as she squeezed him again. "Thank you for finding me."

Lowering his head, his bony cheeks were rosy with a flush Zoe could see even in the moonlight. "All you had to do was call Pith, Miss Zoe. Pith can hear his name when his friends speak it. You should go home now, Miss Zoe. Master Cailean is looking for you...and Master Blaze...and Lazy Bones..."

It killed her to know everyone was probably sick with worry looking for her, especially since they still had to rescue the other women. Being kidnapped three times in a year was truly her luck. A tug of pain arose in her heart, causing her shoulders to slump before her eyes flickered up. "Pith, can you get me out of here?"

The brownie's thin lips spread into a wide smile, each of his yellow teeth gleaming. "Pith is very powerful, Miss Zoe. He can open all the doors with his magic."

Just as hope began to fill her, heavy footsteps approached the cabin from outside. Zoe stiffened, her lungs forgetting how to breathe as the lock clicked and the door swung open.

It wasn't just one silhouette that filled the doorway this time, but two, another taller male standing alongside the one who'd taken her. Zoe's heart stopped as the two men stepped inside, the faint light of the moon revealing their faces. Her captor's eyes gleamed with malice as he smiled, and the man behind him looked at her intently. While her mind searched for an escape, she shrank back, a heavy cloak of fear covering her. She glanced to the side, searching for Pith, but he wasn't anywhere in sight.

"I found you a new mate quicker than I expected, sweetheart," her captor said as he took another step toward her, his voice filled with arrogance. "He's promised to treat you really well."

The words brought bile up her throat, and she instinctively took a step back.

"I don't need a new mate, you piece of shit!" Although Zoe knew mouthing off would only make things more difficult for her, she couldn't help it. "I already have the mate who was meant for me!"

As her captor smirked and reached for her arm, the metal bucket soared through the air of its own accord, hitting him in the face. The crunch of his nose breaking filled the space. Knocked unconscious, he fell to the ground in a heap.

In the moment of confusion that followed, Zoe lunged forward, her fist slamming into the jaw of the taller male, pain instantly radiating up her arm from the force of it. He stumbled back, seeming surprised by her attack, and did not immediately retaliate.

Not wasting any time, she made a break for it, shoving her way past him and sprinting into the woods as fast as her legs could carry her. No footsteps followed, at least none she could hear above the heartbeat that roared in her ears.

Pumped with adrenaline, she ran as if her life depended on it - because it did. With tears streaming down her face, she maneuvered around trees and brush without looking back. The only sounds she heard were her feet hitting the ground.

She was free. Finally, she was free.

Chapter 17

Zoe

After a few miles of running, the pain in Zoe's side and the shortness of her breath forced her to stop and take a break. Nothing she'd passed looked familiar. Having been unconscious during her abduction, she had no idea how far away he had taken her or in what direction.

Lowering herself onto the ground behind the brush, she took deep breaths, hissing as she pulled off her shoes to stretch her sore and bleeding feet. She'd felt the blisters develop, but she had been forced to run through the pain, so she could continue to distance herself from the male who'd stolen her.

"Pith?" Zoe asked, her voice low, not wanting to draw anyone's attention except the brownie she was trying to summon. She had not yet seen Pith reappear since her escape. She realized he was the one who had thrown the bucket. However, she didn't know if he had followed her out of the cabin or if he had left and gone somewhere else. Perhaps he'd returned to Cailean or Blaze and Elianna and told them where to find her. That was her hope, although she had no way of knowing if it would be her reality. Without any water, her mouth was parched, her tongue sticky against the top of her mouth. She realized she couldn't run much farther without something to drink and bandages for her feet.

Heavy footsteps echoed through the forest behind her, and she peeked around the trees to see who it was, praying it was her mate and not her enemy.

As her eyes landed on the male riding on top of a chestnut horse, her breath caught in her throat.

The male who captured her the first time had found her again, but she would rather die than let him take her.

Sucking in a deep breath and pulling her shoes back onto her throbbing feet, Zoe crept around the trees in the opposite direction from where he was headed. Instead of running, she moved slowly and quietly away from him.

The cracking of a branch below her shoe broke through the silence of the forest. She halted where she stood, her heart beating loud enough for the male to hear it. A beat later, before she moved an inch, he called out to her, and the horse's hoof beats sped up, heading in her direction.

"Help me! Someone, please help me!" Zoe screamed as loudly as she could for anyone close enough to hear.

Running as fast as her broken feet could take her, she maneuvered around trees and brush, ducking below low branches and trying to make his path more treacherous. She hoped to slow him down. "Help! Pith, help!"

Quicker than she thought it would've been possible, the fae male caught up to her, his boot slamming into her side before she had a chance to move out of the way.

With a cry of pain, Zoe hit the ground, arms wrapped around her core to protect her rib cage from more abuse. Her tears clouded her eyes as she watched him circle around on his horse. He was no longer in a hurry since he knew she was hurt and would not run away. His eyes gleamed with sadistic pleasure as he surveyed her pain from atop his horse.

"Just leave me alone! Please let me go home to my mate. Please!"

The side of his lip lifted in a cruel smile as he hopped off his horse and sauntered toward her. As if daring her to defy him again, he looked her up and down with amusement.

"I already told you, sweetheart. I have a mate for you. Although I thought I was going to have to find another one for you since you punched the last guy in the face."

He chuckled, pulling a blade from its sheath from his thigh. Zoe scooted back until her back collided with a tree trunk.

"You're lucky he was impressed by your strength and feistiness. He has decided he still wants you."

Bile burned in Zoe's throat as she shook her head vehemently. "You will not touch me again! Neither of you!"

Though Zoe knew Cailean would come for her, she was unsure how long it would take him to find her or what state she would be in when he did. She was sure of one thing - Cailean would stop at nothing to rescue her.

"If your mate wants a female, he can buy one like the rest of us have to do since the keys are a waste of time. How many of us have been to the portal to find our females missing? And that's *if* we ever receive a call at all. Some of us never get a key. We never get the promise of a mate! So, if your male wants a mate, he can wait in line and buy himself one like the rest of us!"

Her body trembled as her eyes searched the forest around her, silently praying for a sign of anyone who could help her. However, she only heard the rustle of leaves as the wind blew. The realization of how helpless she was sent fear creeping up her spine, and her heart sank. She knew she had to find a way out before he took her away again, but she had no weapons, no way to escape.

As a second set of footsteps approached from behind her and the male he'd sold her to came into view, her captor sneered. He took a step toward her, swiping his hand down to grab her arm. Before he touched her, however, a whoosh of air flitted her sweaty hair against her face, and Pith appeared mere inches in front of her, holding a flickering golden key.

Chapter 18

Cailean

Wallflower galloped forward as Cailean followed his instincts, hoping they would lead him to his mate. Elianna and Blaze rode by his side. The couple caught up with him in the forest after meeting up with the other males in town. Although at least a dozen males were now looking for Zoe, Cailean wanted to rescue her. After everything they'd experienced, he didn't trust another male to find her, none other than himself or Blaze. Any male among those could be equally willing to steal another's mate if they wanted one for themselves.

They traveled for hours, heading north and then circling to the west, back in the direction of the Court of Knowledge. Apart from a few abandoned cabins, there had been nothing but trees. Each direction looked the same, making it difficult to determine whether he had passed through the same area more than once. If he and Zoe had been connected by their keys, they would have been able to find each other no matter how much distance spanned between them. However, she'd left the house with no key that morning, and his key never sung to the one she'd had anyway.

"I heard something," Blaze said, holding his finger up to his mouth. Cailean did as instructed, remaining silent as he peeled his ears to listen, even though he did not have gifted hearing like his friend.

Cailean heard nothing other than the sounds of wildlife, but after a few heartbeats, Blaze nodded and pointed forward.

Needing no more direction, Cailean pulled his sword out of its sheath and dug his heels into Wallflower's side, encouraging her to dart ahead. Between the movement of the saddle below him and the heavy beating of his heart, he nearly missed the pulsing sensation of the key in his pocket. It caught him off guard, and confusion swept over him for a moment. Despite not even knowing he had his key on him, it pulsed against his side.

With no intention of slowing Wallflower's progress, Cailean reached into his cloak pocket and pulled out his key, its silver metal flickering impatiently, luring him forward. As he guided his mount in the direction the key led him, it didn't take long for him to hear Zoe's screams.

The forest he found himself in was thick with trees and brush, making it nearly impossible for Wallflower to move quickly. Pulling on the reins, he forced her to stop so he could climb off. Blaze and Elianna dismounted their horse and followed him as he ran into the forest in the direction of his mate's cries for help.

As Cailean found his way around a thick grouping of trees, the first thing he saw was the male looming over his mate, swearing curses and threats at her. Not wanting the enemy to lash out and harm her, Cailean stalked like the skilled hunter he was. He crept around the bushes to get a closer look at Zoe and see what condition she was in. Blaze and Elianna moved slowly in the other direction, creeping through the trees until they were out of sight.

As Zoe lay helpless on the ground, it was clear that she was in pain, but Cailean didn't want to put her at further risk, so he fought the urge to run to her. Taking his breath from his lungs, a golden key flickered in her hand. He knew how she got it in a moment when he realized the only thing standing between her and her attacker was the tiny form of a brownie.

With his arms outstretched, Pith did his best to protect Zoe from being taken against her will. A squeeze of tension arose in Cailean's chest as Pith bravely defended his friend with no sign of fear.

The enemy yelled out, slashing his blade toward the brownie. Before his dagger struck its target, however, it was ripped from his hand by an unseen force and tossed several feet away.

The moment Zoe's attacker was blindsided by his blade stabbing into a tree several feet away, Cailean shot forward out of the brush, striking the other male across the arm with his sword.

His enemy grunted, blood spurting as he reached his hand around to cover the wound. When he turned around to face Cailean, Zoe dashed into the trees, disappearing in the chaos of green. With his arm still spurting blood, the enemy pulled out his sword and held it aloft in Cailean's direction, the weapon trembling in his hand.

"How dare you take my mate from me?" Cailean growled, swiping his sword at the male's throat. However, the injured male leapt out of the way before it made contact.

The enemy snarled as he swung, nearly catching Cailean in the leg. "She's not yours!"

Cailean's attention was briefly caught by the sound of swords clashing as Blaze struggled against another attacker. As Cailean slashed high, trying to catch the enemy in the throat, the other male's sword met his in the air and knocked it out of his hand.

On instinct, Cailean ducked and rolled, avoiding the enemy's strikes. He lunged forward, scrambling for his blade, his fingers digging into the dirt as he gripped the hilt. The other male rushed for him, slashing down to catch him in the back. However, his body stiffened before the attacker could strike as a dagger pierced his chest. Zoe had come out of nowhere, stabbing her attacker with the blade that had flown from his hand.

The enemy fell to the ground, his life leaking into the leaf-littered dirt. With a shaky grip on the dagger, Zoe stepped back, her gaze intense and her breathing labored. Cailean closed the distance between them without wasting a moment and pulled her into his arms. Her body seemed to melt into his embrace, fear and tension ebbing away like the life of their fallen enemy.

As they sat on Wallflower's saddle, Cailean held Zoe close to his chest the entire way back to Blaze's cottage. She could no longer question whether he was her key's choice of a mate, even if she had chosen him herself. Within minutes of her attacker kicking her to the ground, Pith appeared with another key, one that sent a surge of awareness through her body. She knew from the moment the cool metal touched her fingers that it was hers. There was no doubt in her mind that it would call to the male she loved. When she held the new key in her hand, she was certain Cailean would find her.

As Zoe held the enchanted object in her hand, watching the gilded metal flicker and flash against her skin, the loyal brownie stood between her and her attacker, protecting her with his magic until her mate came to her aid. As Pith always said, he was very powerful. Never again would anyone doubt it. Pith had made himself a hero in her eyes, and he would always be treated as a prized family member.

Although she hadn't realized how far away her attacker had taken her, it took them all night to return home. It wasn't until the sun peeked over the horizon that they spotted the cottage. Having been taken so far from Cailean, she realized she might not have been found without the key. It turned her stomach to think about it. She hugged the key close to her chest. In the darkness, its weight felt like a talisman, protecting her. It had brought her home.

No less than twenty fae were waiting for them when they arrived on Blaze's property. A bonfire was burning in the center of his yard, with tents set up around it. Despite their presence, she paid them no attention because she'd already suffered enough. The last thing she wanted to do was see strangers for a while. So, as Blaze and Elianna headed to greet the newcomers and let them know that Zoe had been found, Cailean lifted her off the horse's back, carrying her inside. It was clear that Cailean was not taking any chances that night. Once he had her in his arms, he didn't let her go.

"Food or bath?" he asked as he stood in the center of the living room, holding her like a baby in his arms. Exhaustion made the decision for her, and she dipped her head in the direction of their bedroom.

After fighting for her life and drawing blood for the first time, she wasn't hungry. Even though she had never intended to kill her captor, she had done just that. While he may have deserved it, she knew it would haunt her for the rest of her life. Though she knew she would not face legal action in the fae world, she wasn't sure what options she would have if her actions kept her awake at night. In the fae world or not, guilt remained. Her only hope was that those she loved would be able to help her through it, just as they would help Elianna through her trauma.

It was likely that all of the women captured at the portal had been damaged in some way, not only from being imprisoned and abused, but also from facing their own mortality and separation from their families and worlds. They all had something to work through, and Zoe knew that when they did rescue the other women, they would all need to get through it together. With all the strength they showed in their time together, she knew they would be able to do it.

Walking into their suite, Cailean bypassed the bed and brought her into the bathroom, setting her down on the stool next to the tub.

As he prepared her water, he took such care to make sure the temperature was comfortable and smelled of lavender. His thoughtful gestures warmed her heart, and her love for him grew. She ached to be held by him, wrapped in his arms for a long time, and letting the rest of the world go by.

When Zoe's bath was ready, he guided her into the tub, and she slipped down, allowing the warm water to soothe her. Her mate never left her side, pouring water over her body and gently washing her from head to toe without expecting her to say anything at all. Her mind needed a break. She needed time to process what had happened to her and to remind herself that it was over.

As his hands moved, her whole body relaxed, feeling grateful for his presence. She was overwhelmed with relief - the loving care of her mate made her feel protected and safe, reminding her that the trauma of the past was over, and she could finally begin to move on. When he finished, he wrapped her in a towel and carried her to the bedroom, tucking her in and stroking her face until she fell asleep.

"We should get back outside while they discuss the plan," Cailean said, but his mischievous grin said otherwise. Zoe leaned in close and kissed him, her fingers slipping into his silky, dark hair. The king's forces had arrived that morning, preparing to return to the Court of Knowledge to wage war on Lord Argall and his supporters, but Zoe had no interest in getting out of bed. Not yet, at least.

The first few days following her rescue, she had wanted nothing more than to hold him, but that had changed quickly. As soon as the numbness left her chest, her body had been on fire for him, and she hadn't been able to quench the thirst, despite their best efforts. Since her mind had calmed again, they'd spent a lot of time tangled up in sheets together.

"I think Blaze, the forty or so armed males looking for their mates, and all the king's men can handle it without us." She pressed her lips against his neck, feeling his skin heat up beneath her touch. "Let's stay in bed for a bit longer."

He chuckled, wrapping his arms around her back and pulling her on top of him. For the first time in several mornings, Pith hadn't roused them to clean their room. Zoe wanted to take full advantage of the erection that her mate had woken up with while they had privacy. As she settled on top of him, the full length of his cock lined up against her center. She ground against it, the friction forcing a moan from her lips.

"Maybe for just a little while," he said, his voice filled with need as his breath fanned over her lips.

With his arms around her, Cailean flipped her onto her back and pressed his lips to hers again, his tongue dipping in to taste her. His skin was warm, and his body was such a solid weight over her, his masculine scent making her want to roll him over and lick him from head to toe. They didn't have time for that, but she intended to do it when they did. For now, before she was forced to mix with dozens of strangers, she just wanted him inside her. She wanted him to fill her

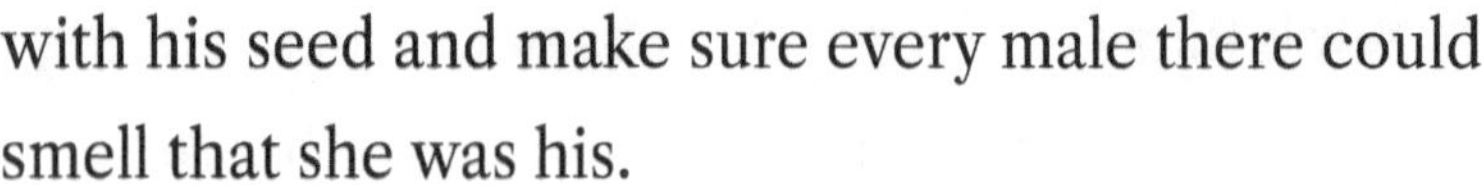

with his seed and make sure every male there could smell that she was his.

Pressing his mouth to hers again, Cailean took a moment to slide his cock through her wetness, ensuring she was ready for him before gliding inside. The way her body stretched to fit him was exquisite, as was how he rolled his hips against hers, his every surge into her setting her senses ablaze.

"Harder," she breathed, her nails digging into the muscles of his backside. "Please."

Nostrils flaring, his dark eyes held her gaze as he slid his hand down to grip her hip.

Zoe's head fell back as he started to move, breath squeezing in her lungs as the coil tightened in her belly. Fire burned in her veins as the pleasure rose and raced through her, a wave of intensity threatening to consume her.

Cailean's thrusts were punishing, hard and deep, breaking the coil into a million pieces as his lips swallowed her screams.

He kissed her, pushing her further into the mattress as he joined her in bliss, burying his face in her neck as he released inside her. The rhythm of his heart beat in time with hers as they held each other close.

As she lay in the bed, cuddling against him as her breathing slowed, she couldn't help but think about her friends back at the lord's manor and those spread around the continent. There were fifty-seven keys in Blaze and Elianna's bedroom, and more than forty males scattered throughout the property, waiting to rescue their mates. Zoe realized that it would be a long road for them to reunite every couple, but she hoped they would be able to. All of her friends deserved the happiness that she and Elianna had found. Although the upcoming fight filled her with fear, she knew she had to do everything she could to keep the promise she'd made to her friends.

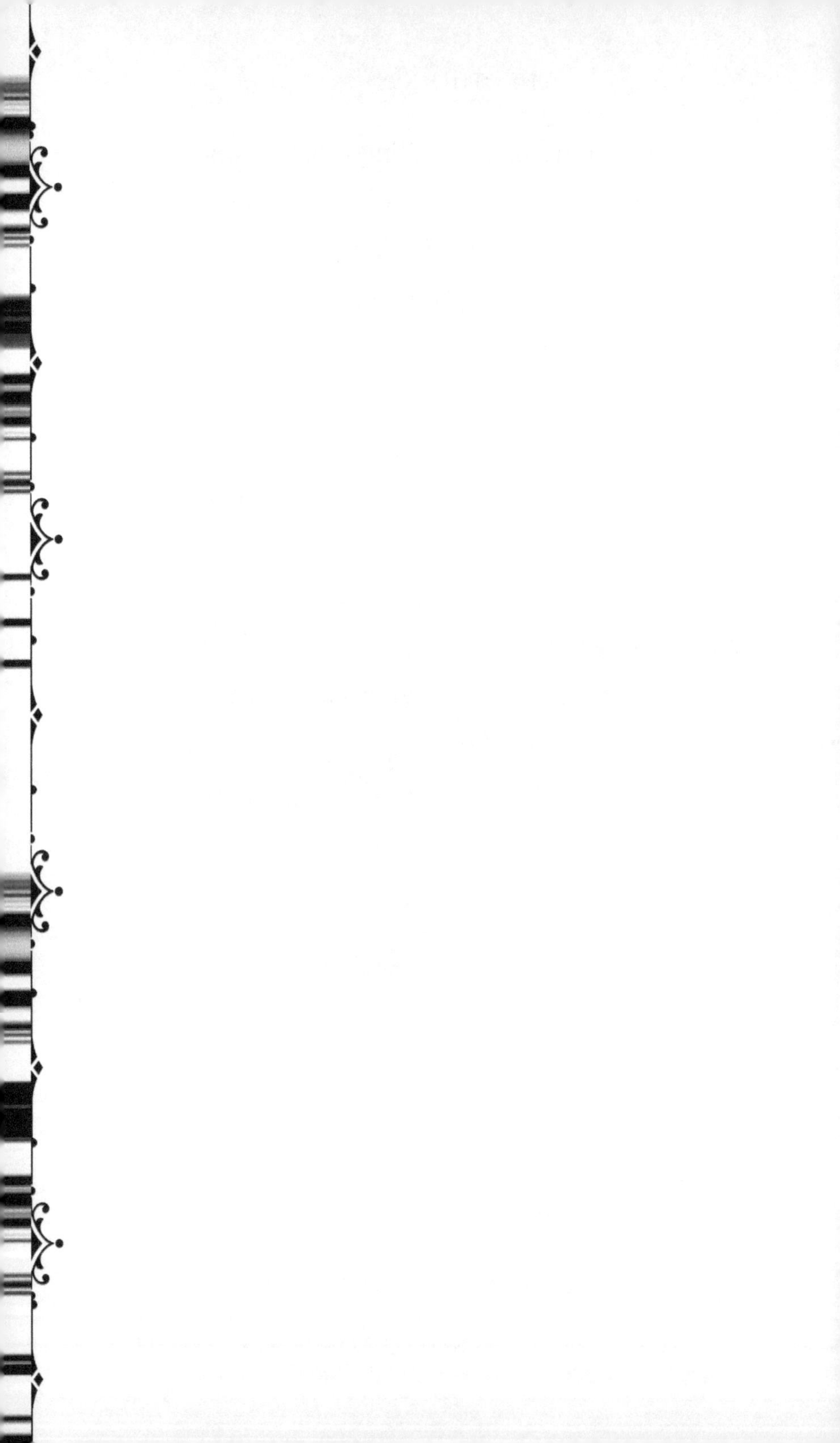

The Story Continues...

Zoe and Elianna have found their happily ever after, but there are still dozens of human women who deserve theirs! More stories are to come!

Book 3, The Other Fate, coming soon.

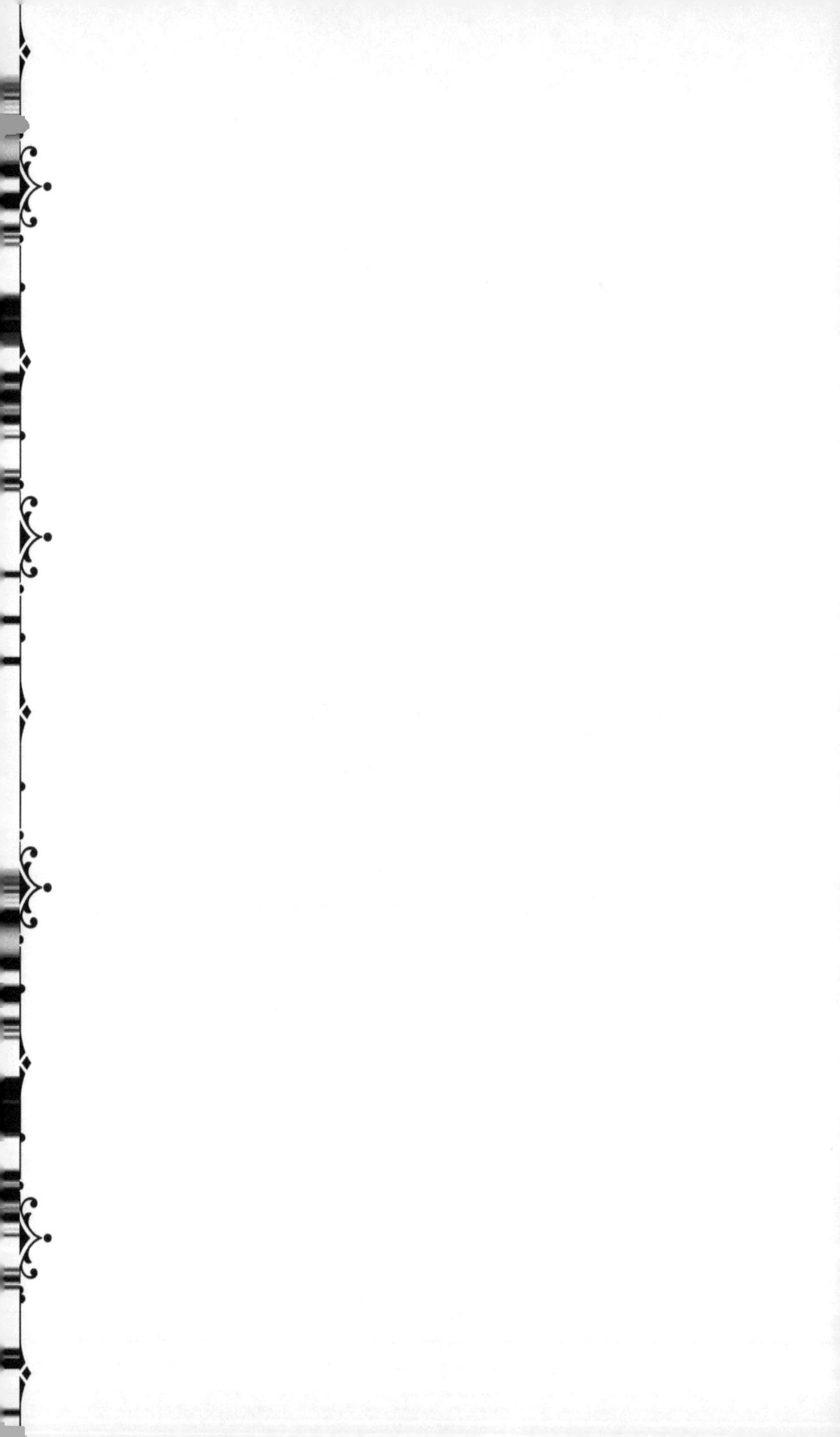

Enjoyed The Other Key?

If you enjoyed this book, don't forget to
leave a review!

Reviews are vital to authors! They
help books reach new readers. I really
appreciate it!

Leave a review here:
https://www.amazon.com/dp/B0BDY15761

CROWN OF THE PHOENIX

BOOK ONE

C. A. VARIAN

INAS

Breqan
El-Wahba
Kotol
Monen
Illever
Harmuz Sea
Howling Forest
Marella Arch
Vaekros

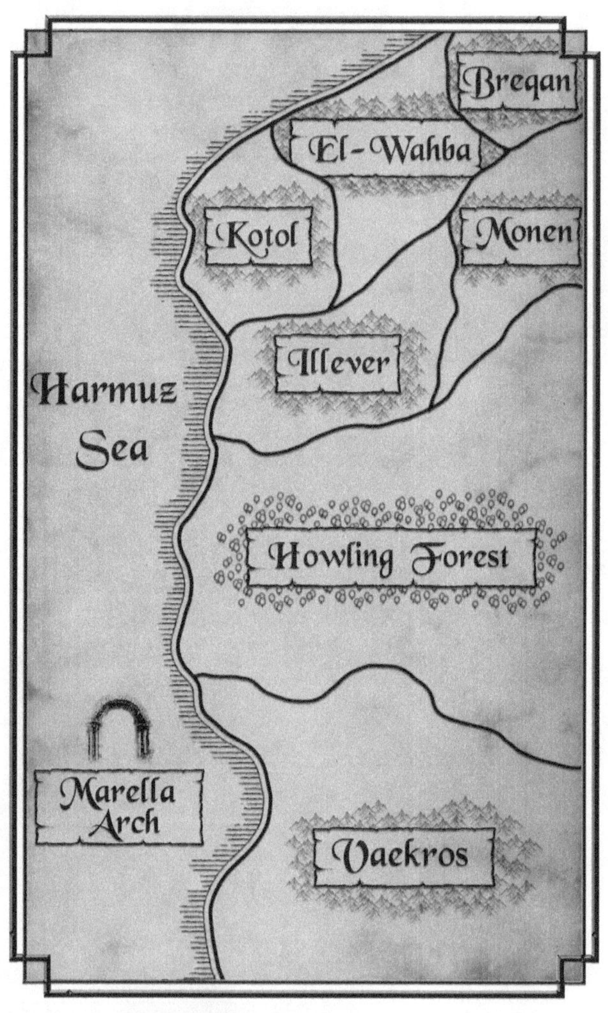

EKOTORIA

Aegricia
Marella Arch
Norithae
Spectre Forest
Elder Sea
Undying Desert
Diapolis
Warbotach

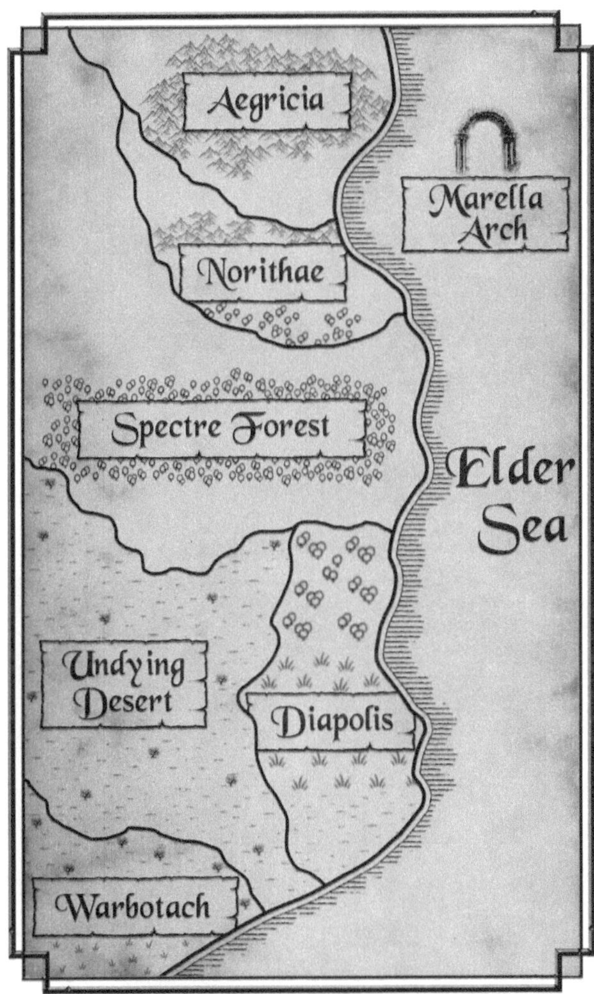

Chapter 1

Vaekros

Blood thrashed her veins like it wished to erode her very being, much like the sea upon the rocky shoreline. Pain unlike anything she'd ever known raged within her as she felt the call. She wanted—needed—to go to the arch. The irresistible longing was an unbearable weight on her chest, sharpening each breath, and telling her to fly.

"Aurelia, you're going to have to try harder if you're ever going to be able to defend yourself. You hit like a girl!"

Wiping the sweat off her brow, Aurelia Vesta grasped her sword in both hands, swinging at Amadeus' larger weapon, only for him to slap hers to the ground. She grunted.

"It's not a fair fight, you know. Your blade is bigger."

Her brother snorted, bracing his feet in a defensive stance.

"Likely excuse, Lia. Likely excuse."

"Room for me?" Septima strolled across the grounds of the villa, calling out to them. Just as Amadeus turned to look at their sister, Aurelia slammed her sword into his, forcing it from his hands. It clattered loudly as it hit the grass.

"Hey!" His outraged shriek held little threat with Aurelia's blade now leveled with his gut. "I wasn't ready."

Waiting until she thought he just may piss himself, she smirked and lowered her weapon to her side. "Likely story, Amadeus. Likely story."

Dropping her sword, Aurelia ran to Septima, wrapping her arm around her sister's shoulder. "We have room for you, but I doubt you want to fight against that loser." She flipped her thumb over her shoulder, pointing at their brother, who rolled his eyes.

"I'll fight you then," Septima said as she darted for Amadeus' sword, swiping it from the ground, and wielding it in her sister's direction.

Aurelia retrieved her blade and swung it at Septima, only for her strike to be blocked. Her jaw dropped as Septima sneered at her. When her look morphed into a mischievous one, Aurelia braced herself for retaliation.

Amadeus began walking toward the house. "I'm going to head home. I'll grab my sword later. Have fun and try not to cut off each other's ears."

The sisters barely paid attention to him as their eyes remained on one another, waiting for the next move to be taken. Septima circled left, waving her weapon in arcs. Aurelia backed up, dropped her weapon on the ground, and took off running toward the gardens. She was tired of sparring, and leading a chase was far more fun. Glancing over her shoulder, she noticed Septima in pursuit.

Once they entered the gardens, the pair fell to the ground and began giggling uncontrollably. They laid among the flowers, admiring the cloudless sky and the breeze rolling off the Harmuz Sea. The sea, ever crashing against the weather-beaten white cliffs, carved dramatic rock faces. Though the cliffs were too high to climb down for a swim, the view was magnificent. Laying in the gardens, overlooking the water below, was one of their favorite pastimes.

"It must be such a thrill," Septima said, rolling onto her side to face Aurelia. Her dark eyes shined in the sunlight and her long ebony braids shimmered like black silk.

Aurelia turned to face her sister, twirling a yellow wildflower between her fingers. "What would be a thrill?"

The longing for adventure played across Septima's features. "To fight... to be a badass warrior. I'm sick of being expected to be a proper lady who spends her time doing tedious things."

Sighing, Aurelia flicked the flower toward her sister. It landed near her hand. "Father would never allow it. You know we are to be wed. It's what is expected of us. I'm surprised he hasn't married me off yet. My twenty-first birthday will be here soon." She knew why her sister wanted to seek adventure instead of marriage, but she did not know how to help to make that happen for her. It was something she thought about often, knowing Septima did not fancy men at all. She was only attracted to women, but marrying the same sex was not allowed in Vaekros. Neither were women warriors. The options to bring her sister happiness were slim, and that was heartbreaking.

Rolling her eyes, Septima turned onto her back to gaze at the sky. "I'm not getting married to a man, expectations or not."

Aurelia's chest tightened at her sister's plight. "Marrying a woman isn't an option in Vaekros. You know that."

Septima sighed. "That may be true, but I will not be forced to marry a man, either. I'd rather die, Lia. I will not do it."

Aurelia bit her lip and turned to stare at the sky as well. They laid in silence for a while, neither knowing how to continue the conversation. Neither knowing how to solve a problem that had no solution in their society.

Aurelia stood and dusted off her clothes. "I'm going to go check on Kano. He needs to get out of the house before he shreds up everything in it. I'll catch up with you a bit later." She leaned over to give her sister a kiss on the cheek before heading toward the house. Septima waved as she walked away.

While Septima was not Aurelia's sister by blood, she was the single most important person in her life. Aurelia's father had found Septima when she was only a baby, while his army laid siege on El-Wahba. Septima's father had been killed in the attack, and her mother had been enslaved. Aurelia's parents became Septima's, although they could not have been more different in appearance.

Septima was not the only baby their father saved and brought back to their home in Vaekros. He had also given Aurelia a tiger cub. Her beautiful Kano who, aside from Septima, was her best friend. She remembered it like it was yesterday. She was less than two years old when she met her baby sister, but was ten years old when the tiny cub was placed in her arms. She named him after the Sun God, because the colors of his fur reminded her of that golden orb in the sky. No one thought he would survive—a runt they called him—but she had cared for him, and he grew and thrived. Some would shun such a pet, but Kano was far kinder than his wild kin. For ten years, he had grown with, loved, and protected her.

Aurelia approached the villa from the back door. She adored the home. It was disposed dramatically along the rocky cliff tops near the Howling Mountains and Forest. The large seaside estate, decorated with mosaics and frescoes, was built around an outdoor atrium. The external walls were covered in stones and a separate building housed the servants. A small wooden cottage on the edge of the property belonged to Amadeus, who had yet to be married.

The stone atrium was filled with a variety of potted trees, vines, and flowers. A large pool sparkled in its center—a pool the girls frequented in the warmer months since reaching the sea was impossible from the height of the house.

Inside the stately villa, sleeping chambers, guestrooms, bathing rooms, reception areas, dining rooms, and even a library filled the large, two-level home. The floors were polished marble and gleamed throughout the structure. Her father, Proteus, made sure of it. He did not allow a dirty house, and the servants knew better than to disobey him. So did his children. His decades as military commander reinforced his no-nonsense personality. There was no warmth in Proteus. Aurelia wondered if he had always been that way, or if the death of her mother changed him.

When Aurelia entered her bedchamber, Kano stretched his massive body and slinked up to her to nuzzle her legs. She dropped into the vanity seat and untangled her braid while she gazed at herself in the bronze mirror. Her large blue eyes and crimson hair were such a contrast to Septima's long midnight braids and her deep tawny skin.

Some said her red hair was a gift from Veena, the Goddess of Life and Death. Not unlike the goddess, Aurelia loved to spar. She loved learning to wield weapons, even if it was all but forbidden in her society. She had to be a respectable Vaekrosan lady and that meant never making a man feel weak in her presence. Even so, she sparred with her brother, and with Septima, to practice her swordsmanship. With as many fights as Vaekros picked, she never knew when such skills would be useful.

Aurelia turned to admire her bedchamber. Walls of rich aqua mirrored the color of the sea that always reflected the light of the sun from the floor to ceiling windows. Bright white silk drapes fluttered in the breeze. A huge four-poster bed took up a large part of the suite, large enough for Kano to sleep alongside her and keep her warm.

Her favorite view from her window was that of the Marella arch. The sea had carved an arch out of the rock that looked like a portal to a magical world. The legends of the arch were contradictory in Vaekros, so Aurelia settled on the one in her dreams. The water was too dangerous for anyone to approach it, although

Aurelia dreamed of traversing the distance, of flying through the arch.

Curled up like a mountain at her feet, Kano let out a mighty snore. She reached over and caressed his sleek fur, rousing him from his slumber. Large canines gleamed as he yawned. His amber eyes were still full of sleep. Rising to his feet, he rubbed against the cloth of her pants as she rubbed his head.

"You're being lazy today, Kano. I think it's time for us to play outside."

He bobbed his head like he understood her. Leaving her chambers with the great cat trailing behind her, Aurelia took the stairs quickly to look for Septima and sunshine.

After searching the villa twice over, she found both at the same time. Septima sat on a stone bench in the rose garden, soaking in the sun and reading a book. Kano sprinted at the sight of her, nuzzling his enormous head against Septima's legs. She giggled, ruffling his fur.

"Hey there, big guy," she said, placing a kiss on his head before gleaming a toothy grin at Aurelia. "What are you two up to?"

Aurelia shrugged, dropping to sit beside her. "Kano has been too lazy today. I thought a game of hide and seek would be good for him. Do you want to play?"

Septima chuckled. "Aren't we a little old for such games?"

Rising from the bench, Aurelia straightened her tunic. "I'm older, and I still play." She shrugged. "Let's go Kano, the last one in the forest is a horse's ass."

Running as fast as she could, Aurelia darted into the tree line. The sound of Kano's enormous paws thudded close behind her.

The forest was vast, dense, and rich. Its canopy comprised pine, Buxus, and holly. Enough light shimmered through their crowns for a medley of shrubs to take advantage of the fertile grounds below. Silent vines suspended from many a tree, and a range of flowers, which grew in a sprinkled, disorderly fashion, brightened up the otherwise homogeneous scenery. A mishmash of noises, predominantly those of critters, echoed throughout, and were backed by the occasional sounds of birds of prey gliding in the air.

Aurelia laughed as she ran, climbing into an abandoned hollow just big enough for her to fit. Holding her breath, she knew he could smell her, but he seemed to pretend he couldn't, like he knew the rules of the game.

Quick footsteps paced in the distance. She pulled herself as far into the tree as she could, hoping there weren't any rodents nesting in there that would bite her like last time.

"Got you!" Septima's mane fell into the hollow, nearly slapping her in the face. They both began giggling as Kano bounded up to them as they kneeled, licking their faces.

Aurelia wiped the slobber off her cheek with the back of her hand. "I thought you were too old for this game?"

Septima shrugged as she wiped her own face. "You know I'll be playing in the forest with you even when my hair turns gray, especially with this big guy." She reached out and scratched Kano behind his ear. He leaned into her.

They played for hours. Each taking great care in where they hid, only for Kano to find them each time.

With barely enough energy to walk back to the villa, thirsty and covered in dirt and leaves, the sisters and Kano entered the back garden of their home just as the sun began making its descent over the Howling mountains.

A snarl ripped out of Kano before they cleared the threshold of the house. Aurelia looked at him to see that his ears were laid nearly flat against his head. She gently stroked his fur in an attempt to soothe him. She looked up to see her father standing in the foyer with two strange men, and her heart dropped.

Chapter 2

Aegricia

Walking back to her cell in the depths of the dungeon, Otera dragged her feet as the cloaked monstrosity of a man yanked her alongside him. It was cold—bone chilling—yet she had been pulled out of her bed with little more than a nightdress on. Her people were scared, and her military was gone. She was powerless to help even herself.

"You don't have to drag me. I can walk by myself." She tried to muster power in her voice, but it came out as a desperate plea. He grunted and tugged her arm harder, his fingers biting into her flesh.

She had rarely used the dungeons below her castle. Only the most dangerous criminals were housed there, and only if another punishment was not more fitting. Because the cells received little use, they weren't fit to house anyone, not a dog, and certainly not a person. It was the last place the Aegrician queen ever thought she would find herself.

The Warbotach cavalry had moved swiftly, laying siege to her castle and leaving her with no choice but to let them in or risk harm befalling innocent civilians. Her military had fled, not to abandon their people, but to build up strength and allies. They would then return to Aegricia, when the time was right, and reclaim their land.

That was the plan they settled on when word of the invasion of Norithae had reached them weeks prior. Her warriors would be back for her, for their people, but she did not know when. Until then, the Warbotach leader, Uldon, wanted her power and her crown. He couldn't get it by killing her, so her safety was guaranteed, although her comfort was not.

Forced back into the stone-enclosed darkness, Otera retreated to the straw bed in the cell's corner, as her escort slammed the iron door behind her. The resounding echo, highlighted only by the retreating footsteps of her captor's man, faded into an ominous silence. She had never felt so utterly alone, with only the light of one slender window to keep her company. The light of the window and her endless thoughts.

Chapter 3

Vaekros

Proteus took one look at the dirt on his daughters' clothes and frowned. Not hiding the disdain on his face, he cleared his throat, took a sip from his glass, and gestured toward the stairs. His expression was unyielding, leaving no room for argument. "Aurelia... Septima... go make yourselves presentable and come introduce yourselves to the men you will marry."

Aurelia's lungs lost their ability to expand, and she saw the same look of dread color on her sister's face. Septima wrapped her arms around her chest as they locked eyes, before they forced their feet upon the steps. The pair climbed higher, feeling as though they were walking to their deaths. Instead of heading to her own chambers, Septima followed Aurelia.

"I can't do this, Lia," Septima said, as she pulled her filthy clothes over her head. She scurried through the bathing room that separated their chambers to grab a suitable dress. "I will not marry that man."

Aurelia's heart hammered as she stepped out of her trousers, tripping over the fabric as her chaotic thoughts whirled. "I know. We'll figure this out. I promise. But we have to go back downstairs."

Septima grimaced as she tied her dress into place, ignoring her disheveled hair, and walked toward the door. Aurelia followed.

Stumbling down the stairs to the strange men who waited for their hands in marriage, both women silently begged for a way out.

As they entered the dining room, they saw their father and the two men sitting at the table with glasses of brown liquor in their hands. Both men looked to be in their late twenties, nearly a decade older than their potential brides. The sisters took the seats opposite the suitors, with Proteus at the head of the table—a king in his castle. Proteus' face held no humor or patience for their objections, and the sisters knew better than to raise any.

Aurelia glanced at the vacant chair opposite their father, where their mother sat before she passed away. Although it had been nearly fifteen years, Aurelia's heart still ached when she looked at that empty seat.

She had always imagined her mother being at her wedding and teaching her to care for her children when the time came. Instead, it was servants and nannies who raised her while Proteus fought in wars and spent his time in the Vaekrosan Senate, which was days away in the capital city of Westtide.

Her mother, Messalina, had succumbed to the plague. Her father, having been away on campaign in a foreign land, was not infected. Aurelia and Septima, only children then, were also spared, kept away at the first sign of illness. Aurelia didn't have to watch her mother waste away, a fact that comforted her. She had loved her mother dearly and was glad to keep the memories of her beautiful face in her mind, not her deathly visage.

"Aurelia," Proteus said, interrupting her thoughts. "I'd like you to meet Philo."

The man directly across from her dipped his head in acknowledgement as a half-smile spread across his face. "Nice to meet you," he said.

"And you," she responded, forcing a smile of her own, although she knew it did not reach her eyes.

Philo was handsome, but he was at least five or more years her senior. Sandy blond hair swept across his forehead but was pulled back into a ponytail at his nape. His eyes, the color of summer grass, eased her nerves ever so slightly. She didn't want to marry him; she didn't even know him, but she was relieved that he at least appeared to be kind.

"Septima," her father said, motioning to the other man. "I'd like you to meet Caius."

Her sister's ashen face pinched in a nauseated grimace as she looked at Caius. He greeted her kindly, but she did not appear to be interested. Aurelia knew better. After breathing what appeared to be a hello, Septima reached for Aurelia below the table. Lacing their fingers together, Aurelia ran her thumb over Septima's trembling hand. The air in the room felt too thin as she struggled to inhale.

Caius was also an attractive man, though that meant nothing to her sister. Philo was fair like Aurelia, but Caius' complexion was bronzed. With his dark hair, rich brown eyes, and sun-kissed skin, Aurelia assumed he was from the city of Kotol.

Proteus rambled on with the men, not taking a moment to acknowledge his daughters or inquire about their wishes. He didn't bother to even ask about their day.

Dinner was brought out as Aurelia and Septima sat in silence, watching their father talk with the two men.

Roasted duck and vegetables were placed in front of them as well as a tomato and cream bisque. The soup was Septima's favorite, but she did not accept the bowl when Aurelia pushed it toward her. Aurelia ate a small amount of each dish, but she had lost her appetite after being accosted at the door by their father with unwanted engagements.

Septima's hand continued to grip Aurelia's, although the tremble had subsided. Aurelia couldn't help but dwell on what her sister was going through at that moment. What would she do if forced to marry a man? Aurelia didn't want to marry a stranger either but marrying for love in Vaekros was unheard of. Still, it was a dream she had always held in her heart, a hope for their society to change.

Most marriages in their world were arranged for purely political reasons. The potential to gain power and connections was the only thing that mattered. Fathers arranged their daughters' unions, usually as soon as they reached eighteen years of age, to someone who could advance the families' political futures. If the bride's family was of a lower class than the groom's, a dowry would be paid to entice the prospective suitor.

Aurelia did not know what arrangement Proteus had made with the two men, but he did not need money or political power. She assumed the arrangement was, at the very least, mutually beneficial to the two families. Although she couldn't imagine it would be beneficial to her or her sister. Philo caught her eye several times, smiling kindly at her. Maybe she could grow to love him, but her sister could not do the same with her own betrothed. Even if she could come to care for him as a person, she would never be able to love him as a wife should.

Their father cleared his throat loudly as they finished dinner. Aurelia frowned. Septima's dish remained untouched. Proteus noticed the full plate but allowed the servant to take it away. The scraps would undoubtedly go to Kano, who was sleeping in the bedroom upstairs.

Rising from the table, her father lowered his eyebrows and leveled them with a stern look that left no room for argument.

"Well," He reached over to shake the suitors' hands. "I have some work to get to in my study. Lydia will bring out dessert. Girls," he said, looking at his daughters. Aurelia's stomach tied in a knot as she hung on Proteus' next words. She didn't want to entertain the men, although it didn't appear she had a choice. She held Proteus' gaze as Septima dropped her head and rubbed her eyes. "Get to know these fine young men. I'll be in my study if anyone needs me."

Nodding to the men he had selected for his daughters', their father strolled out of the dining room.

Once he was gone, Septima rose from the table without warning and dashed out of the room. Proteus would be furious when he found out Septima had abandoned her betrothed at the table. There was no way he would not see her with his study being so near their chambers. Murmuring an apology to the men, Aurelia went to look for her sister.

A loud clap echoed around her as she took the stairs two at a time. Aurelia made it to the second-floor landing as Proteus entered his study.

She found Septima curled up on her bed, sobbing into Kano's fur. He looked up as Aurelia entered the room, but Septima never looked up as sobs wracked her frame. Crawling onto the bed, Aurelia laid behind her sister and wrapped her in an embrace.

"Are you okay?" Aurelia knew she was not okay, but she had no other words for her sister. Proteus didn't have to hit her, but he did a lot of things he didn't need to.

"I can't do this, Lia." Septima's voice hitched as she spoke into Kano's fur. Aurelia squeezed Septima's arm, unsure what to say or do to ease her pain.

"I know, sissy. I just don't know how to fix it."

Septima rolled over onto her back, staring at nothing while she continued to pet Kano. It was more to soothe herself than him. Tears trailed down her beautiful face as the mark from Proteus' hand had begun to turn purple on her cheek.

"I can't stay here. I can't let him do this to me. I don't know where I'll go, but it won't be here."

Aurelia swallowed thickly around the lump of emotion in her throat. "What do you mean? You can't... but..." She fell silent, although her mouth continued to move. Septima turned to face her. Unspeakable sadness was reflected in her eyes.

"I'm sorry. I have to leave. I'm not sure where I'll go. Maybe I'll cross through the forest and go to one of the towns on the other side. I don't know. I just have to get out of this marriage."

Aurelia stewed on her sister's words, trying to make sense of the situation. She couldn't lose her. It wasn't an option. They laid in silence as the sun fell behind the mountains, throwing the room into darkness. As Aurelia rose from the bed to light a candle, dangerous thoughts flooded her mind. Thoughts she was willing to entertain for Septima.

"I'm coming with you."

Septima's eyebrows rose as she lifted herself onto her elbow. "You don't have to sacrifice your own marriage for me."

Aurelia snorted, returning to the bed. "I don't even know that guy. I don't know about you, but I have always wanted to marry for love. I want to make my own way. I can't do that under Father's thumb."

A mischievous smile crawled across her sister's face. "I said I wanted adventure, but this may be more than we bargain for. How will we eat? Where will we stay? There are creatures in those woods. How will we protect ourselves?"

Aurelia glanced sidelong at Septima before reaching out to scratch Kano under the chin. "As long as we have this guy, we will be safe. As far as food, we can pack our satchels with as much as we can carry." She pulled two leather bags out of her armoire, tossing one to her sister. "We can figure the rest out as we go."

Septima sat up, grabbing the bag and pulling it against her body. "When do we leave?"

Looking at the clear night outside the window, Aurelia turned to face her sister. "Tonight."

Having never been on their own before, neither sister knew what to expect once they left the safety and comfort of their father's home. But that didn't matter. They were determined to escape the unwanted marriages that awaited them if they remained in Vaekros. They were going on an adventure. If they could avoid being caught, that is.

Chapter 4

Vaekros

S neaking into the kitchens once the servants had turned in for the night, the sisters stuffed their bags with fruits, vegetables, dried meats, and breads. There were wild berries in the forest, and they could learn to hunt if they needed to, but they grabbed what they could to get themselves started. Both strapped their swords to their backs and a dagger around their thighs. They dressed warmly, choosing tunics and trousers and wrapped hooded cloaks over their shoulders.

After returning to take a final look at the bedroom they adored, Aurelia and Septima left the house unnoticed and entered the night air of the back gardens. Both took a fortifying breath and braced for what the forest, and the future, had in store for them. Giving each other a silent nod, they pulled their hoods

before they headed for the forest, Kano following stealthily behind. The sisters crept to the tree line in silence, not wanting to chance waking their brother, who lived in the cottage at the edge of the property.

They didn't have a plan other than traveling west through the forest. They knew there were small towns that bordered the forest, as well as larger cities, including El-Wahba, which was where Septima was born. All they knew existed beyond the forest was war-torn cities, none of which sounded like a place they wanted to live. So, they intended, at least at first, to settle in one of the smaller towns, and learn what they could about what else was out there. Both women had gold and silver coins in their bags, money they had saved over the years, and money Proteus would not miss. They hoped they could support themselves, for a time, with what they had.

The dense brush of the Howling Forest took on a more ominous appearance at night. It had been named the Howling Forest for a reason. A menacing howl sounded in the distance as an owl hooted from above. Aurelia gripped Kano's leash so tightly her hand ached as she flinched at every sound. Septima's held a torch that illuminated their way as they traversed the dense

branches and vines until it finally opened up to an easier path after several miles.

Knowing they couldn't stop for long, but too exhausted to go any further, they stopped in a thicket to rest. Their father would undoubtedly begin a search to look for them after he had servants scour the extensive property. They had little time to rest, but they could afford to sleep until at least first light. They built a small fire and backed themselves against the trunk of a hollowed-out tree. Septima took the first watch while Aurelia attempted to sleep. Kano remained on high alert while they sat in the darkened forest. Aurelia leaned back against the great cat, closing her eyes and waiting for unconsciousness to consume her.

Tendrils of mist recoiled in front of her, beckoning her forward like the inward curl of a finger. Its invitation was seductive, alluring, but the path was dark. Where was it leading her? She did not know.

"What are you doing here?" The woman demanded as she sat upright in the corner. Her trembling hands straightened the hem of her filthy, tattered dress. Dirt

was caked under her nails as though she had tried to claw her way to freedom. "I cannot give you what you want! You're wasting your time."

The man, face hidden in shadows, huffed angrily as he stomped away. "Maybe some more time in the cell will change your mind."

The sparkle of a glittering crown faded into the darkness as the iron door slammed shut. It no longer sat atop the head of the crimson-haired woman, imprisoned in filth. Instead, it floated away in the calloused hand of the stocky man who had stolen her freedom.

Aurelia woke to hands roughly shaking her shoulders, along with the low growling of Kano at her side.

"Lia, someone's coming. Wake up." Septima crouched beside her, whispering in her ear. Rubbing her eyes and shaking off the strange dream, she sat upright and peered into the distance.

"What's going on?"

"The branches cracked, and I heard voices. I put the fire out, but I think it's too late. They'll see the smoke."

Aurelia nodded as she pulled her legs closer to her body, trying to make herself as small as she could. The faint rustling of trees could be heard in the distance and could almost be mistaken for an animal. But the voices... the muffled voices made it clear people were nearby.

The forest was still black. There was no way to know the time, only that it was somewhere past midnight and before sunrise. It was too late to run. Their footfalls and their inevitable stumbling upon the forest floor would make too much noise for them to escape unnoticed. Their only option was to sit quietly and hope the others would pass them. Aurelia's hands were slick with nervous sweat as her heartbeat thundered in her ears, but they sat still, afraid to breathe as they hoped to remain invisible.

The voices grew closer as the sisters huddled together. Aurelia cringed, clutching at her throat as she realized the people would walk right by their hiding place, and there was nothing they could do about it. Kano's own snarling lowered in volume as if he realized they were supposed to be hiding, and not drawing attention to themselves.

"Do you smell that?" A woman whispered. "Hang on, someone is out here."

The sound of dragging metal slithered through the air, setting Aurelia's teeth on edge. Someone had drawn a weapon.

"Who would be out here?" Another female voice asked. The voice spoke louder, more demanding. "We know someone is out here... no sudden movements... just come out nice and slow."

Eyes wide and with no other solution, the sisters looked at each other. Aurelia grabbed Kano by his leash, and they slowly stood from their place behind the trees.

Two women stood on the trail, only feet from them. They were tall and, although the darkness hid most of their features, the glint of moonlight showed the sword in the hands of the blond woman. Aurelia's stomach did a nervous flip, causing the meager food she consumed to rise in her throat.

"We don't mean any harm," Aurelia said, taking the slightest step back as she reached out and took Septima's hand. "We are just hiding from our father. By the morning, we will be on our way."

The woman who was not holding a weapon, tall with long black hair that draped over her shoulders, tilted her head, eyeing the large tiger at Aurelia's side.

"And the beast?" she asked, as she reached toward the handle of a dagger gleaming at her side.

Aurelia gulped, glancing down at Kano before returning her eyes to the women standing before them. "He's not a beast. He's my friend... my pet. His name is Kano. I've raised him since he was a cub. He protects me."

The women looked at each other and lingered for a few agonizing moments, as though they were communicating silently. The same woman spoke. "And when we walk away, you will sic him on us? Have him tear us to shreds?"

Pursing her lips, Aurelia shook her head vehemently. "No, of course not. He's only here to protect me. He will not harm you if you do not harm us."

The other woman, the one with sword in hand, and hair that appeared white in the moonlight, spoke next. "You said you were hiding from your father. Why?"

Septima squeezed Aurelia's hand gently before responding. "Our father intends to marry us off to strange men. We refuse. We are trying to find somewhere else to create a home, to find a place where we can decide our own futures."

The woman snickered. "It's a foolish endeavor. In a world like this, in Vaekros, there is no escaping such a plan. Your father will find you. Women do not have the kind of rights you seek. Not here."

The black-haired woman shot a warning look at her companion. The woman with the sword looked at the ground in a submissive response. There was somewhere else. Aurelia felt it in her bones. She said not here as though there was another place, a place where women had more rights. She chanced to ask.

"My name is Aurelia. This is my sister, Septima." Aurelia lifted her and Septima's intertwined hands. "If you know of a place where we could be free, please tell us." She thought about explaining why Septima could not—would not marry a man—but she did not know of their prejudices, so she didn't.

The woman who held no weapon, clearly of a higher rank, responded first. "My name is Taryn. This is Exie." The woman with the sword nodded. "We knew of a place like that, a place where women had more rights, but it's no longer safe, so it doesn't warrant discussing."

Aurelia frowned. "Where are you from? Are you from Vaekros?" Although it was apparent that the women were not from Vaekros, she still felt it polite to ask instead of assuming.

"We are from a long way away," Exie responded, with no intention of explaining further.

"But you're in Vaekros," Aurelia pressed. "I don't mean to pry. Do you at least know of somewhere safe my sister and I can go? Somewhere we could survive away from our father?"

Taryn arched an eyebrow, looking them both over. "Can you fight?"

Aurelia started, eyes widening as she glanced at her sister. "Fight?"

"Yes. Can you fight? With a weapon? If you can, then I can use you. Maybe." Taryn waited for the sisters' response, shifting her weight and taking a sip of water from her canteen.

Meeting her eyes, Aurelia nodded, as did Septima, but Septima responded. "We train with our older brother. Aurelia trains more, but we both know the basics. We can learn. We will earn our keep. We don't want charity—just a chance to live free."

"There are towns through this forest, but I doubt you would ever make it, even with a tiger. If your father didn't find you first, there are enough beasts in these trees who are the things of nightmares. I do not want your deaths on my conscience. We will take you to our camp, but I'm telling you this once..." Taryn paused, scanning both sisters. "The moment you enter our camp, you cannot return to your old lives. I need to make sure that is something you can handle."

Catching her sister's gaze, Aurelia bit her lip as she weighed their options. She attempted to steady her voice, to fill it with resolve, as she responded. "We will not miss our lives in Vaekros. A part of us will surely miss our brother but staying here isn't worth losing control of our futures."

Nodding, Taryn held out her hand to Aurelia, and they shook to seal the promise. "Very well. Gather your things. Our patrol is ending, and we must return to camp before first light. We need to move before your father's search parties scour this forest looking for you."

There was not much for the sisters to gather. They had brought barely more than the clothes on their backs and the food they'd stuffed in their satchels, but they collected it. Aurelia wrapped Kano's leash around her hand, petting him gently in assurance, before stepping onto the path to follow the two mysterious women deeper into Howling Forest.

They walked for what felt like hours. Aurelia's legs were weak, threatening to fracture beneath her. The brisk chill of the air wasn't enough to stop the sweat that coated her skin from forming. They walked until night began to fade into day. The light of the sun peeked through the openings in the tree cover, but Exie still held her sword at the ready. Braced for what attack—Aurelia did not know.

As they came upon a clearing, the previously buzzing forest fell silent. Eerie. Finally, sheathing her sword, Exie reached for Septima's hand. Septima stared as if it would bite her. She took a hesitant step back. Before Aurelia could ask what was happening, Taryn reached for her hand as well.

"If you want to follow us," Taryn said impatiently, "then you'll have to take my hand and trust me. You can't cross the barrier on your own."

"Barrier?" Aurelia asked, confusion clear in her tone. Fear of the unknown weighed on her, making her exhausted limbs heavier.

Exie smirked, waiting for Taryn to explain.

"There's more to this world than what you can see around you, Aurelia. If you want to see our world, you'll have to take my hand."

In an unspoken agreement, the sisters dropped their interlaced fingers and grabbed the hands of the mysterious women before being led through an invisible barrier into a place unknown.

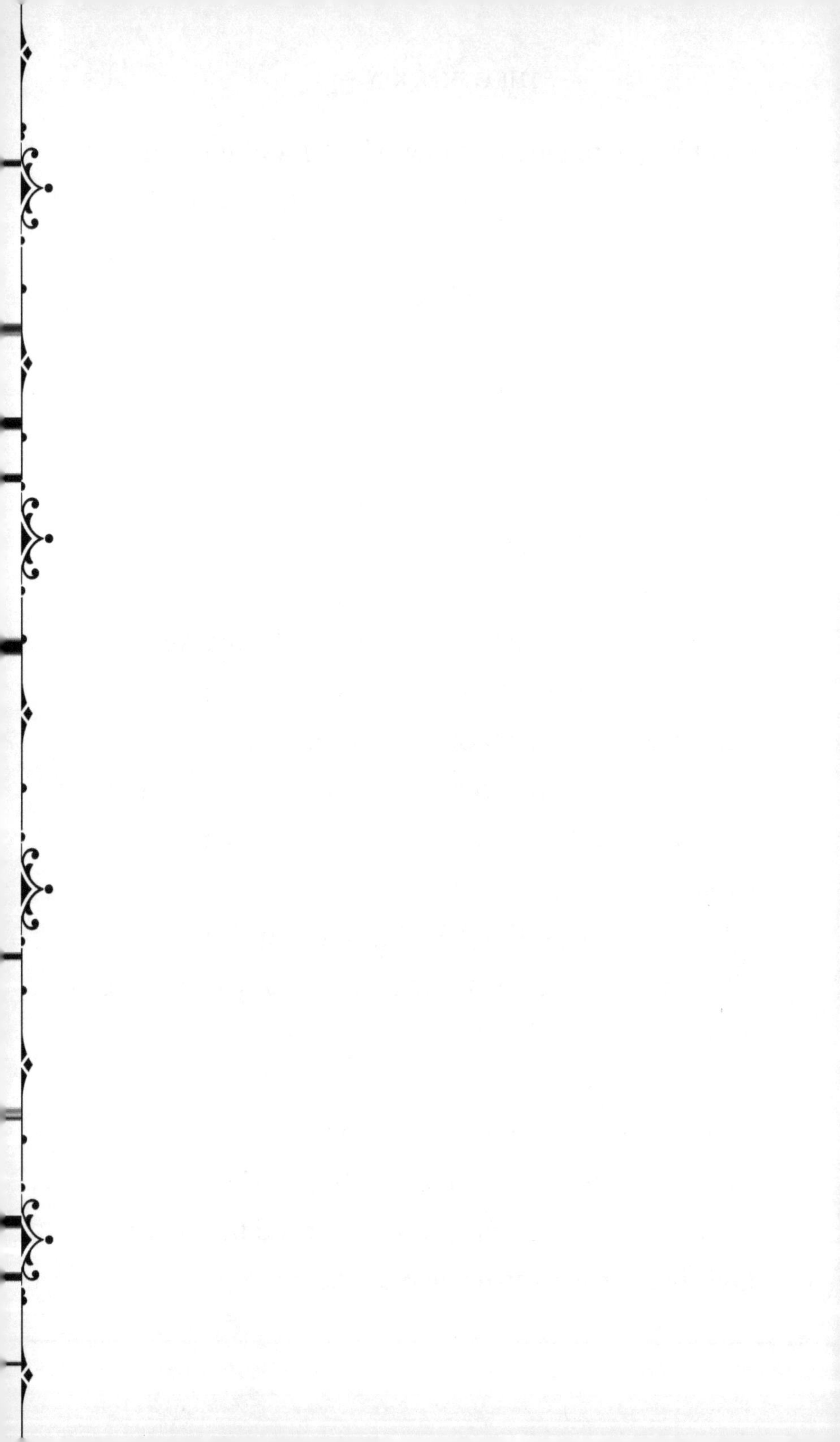

Enjoying Crown of the Phoenix?

Continue the series here:

https://www.amazon.com/dp/B0B258Y1SD

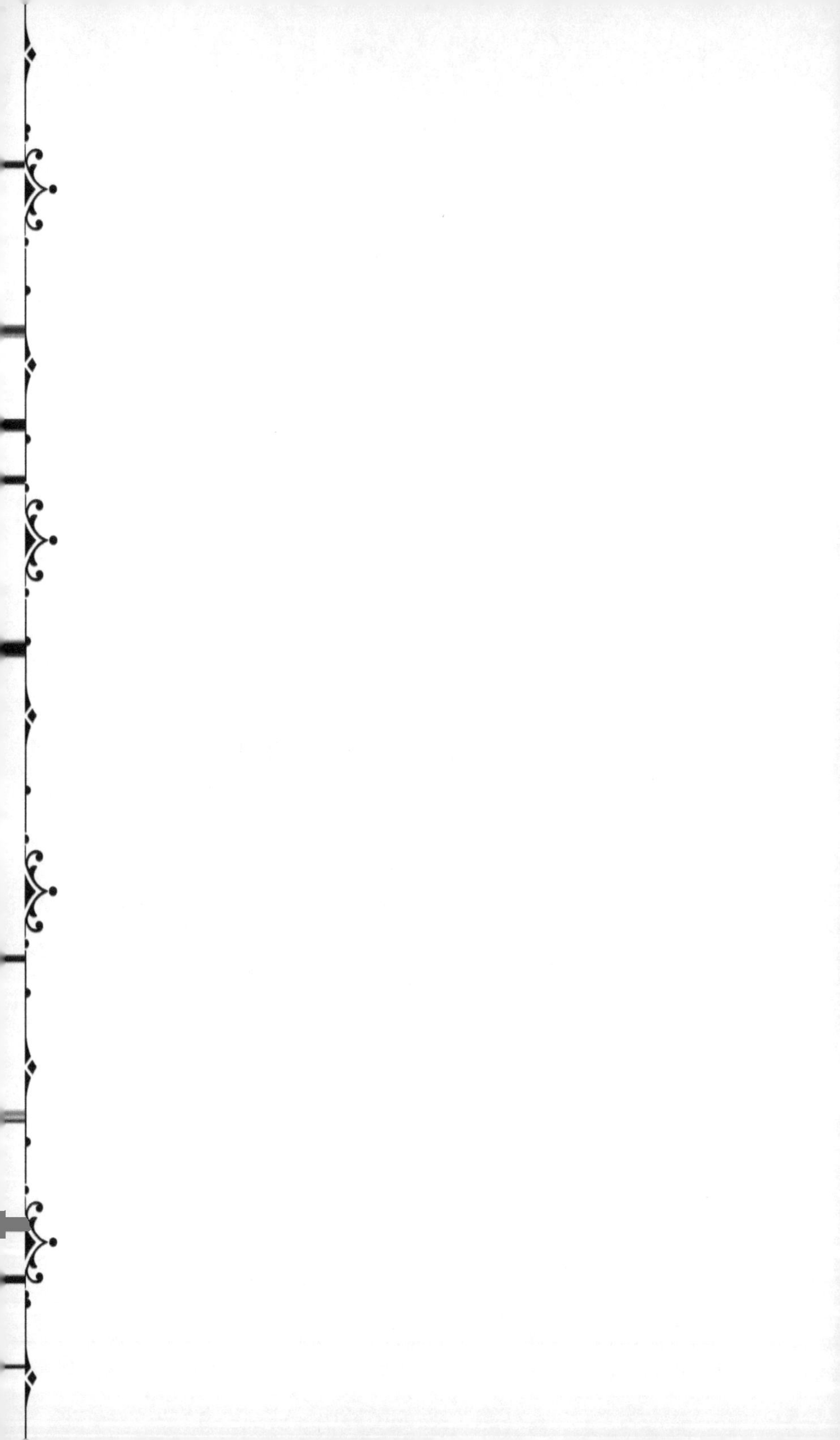

Acknowledgements

I want to thank my editor, Megan, of Willow Oak Author Services for putting up with my crazy editing schedule. (At least I keep the work coming).

I also want to thank Kate Segar for editing this book as well! (and for competing with me on Kindle Vella to keep me motivated).

Thank you to Charlee, of Blurbs, Baubles, and Book Covers, for putting up with me...and formatting my books beautifully...oh yea...and for this and many other covers...my maps too!

My final thank you is to my family, friends, and readers. Thank you for your support.! (Who am I kidding? I have like four friends.)

Also by C. A. Varian

Hazel Watson Mystery Series
Kindred Spirits: Prequel
The Sapphire Necklace
Justice for the Slain
Whispers from the Swamp
Crossroads of Death
Crown of the Phoenix Series
Crown of the Phoenix
Crown of the Exiled
Crown of the Prophecy
Supernatural Savior Series
Song of Death
Goddess of Death
Dozens of stories on Kindle Vella!

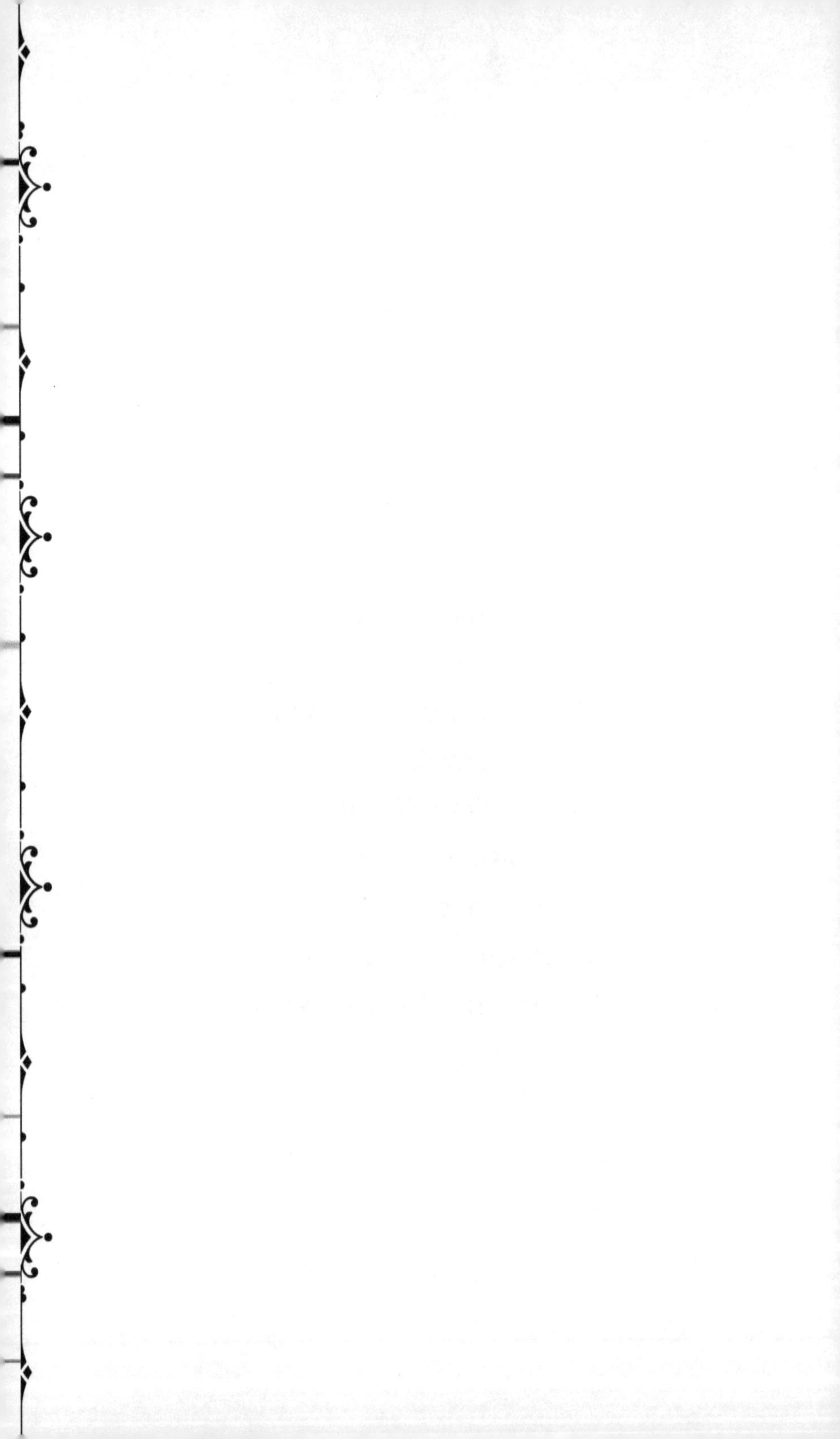

Follow C. A. Varian

Sign up for C. A. Varian's newsletter to receive current updates on her new and upcoming releases, sales, and giveaways: https://sendfox.com/cavarian

You can also find all stories, books, and social media pages and follow her here: https://linktr.ee/cavarian

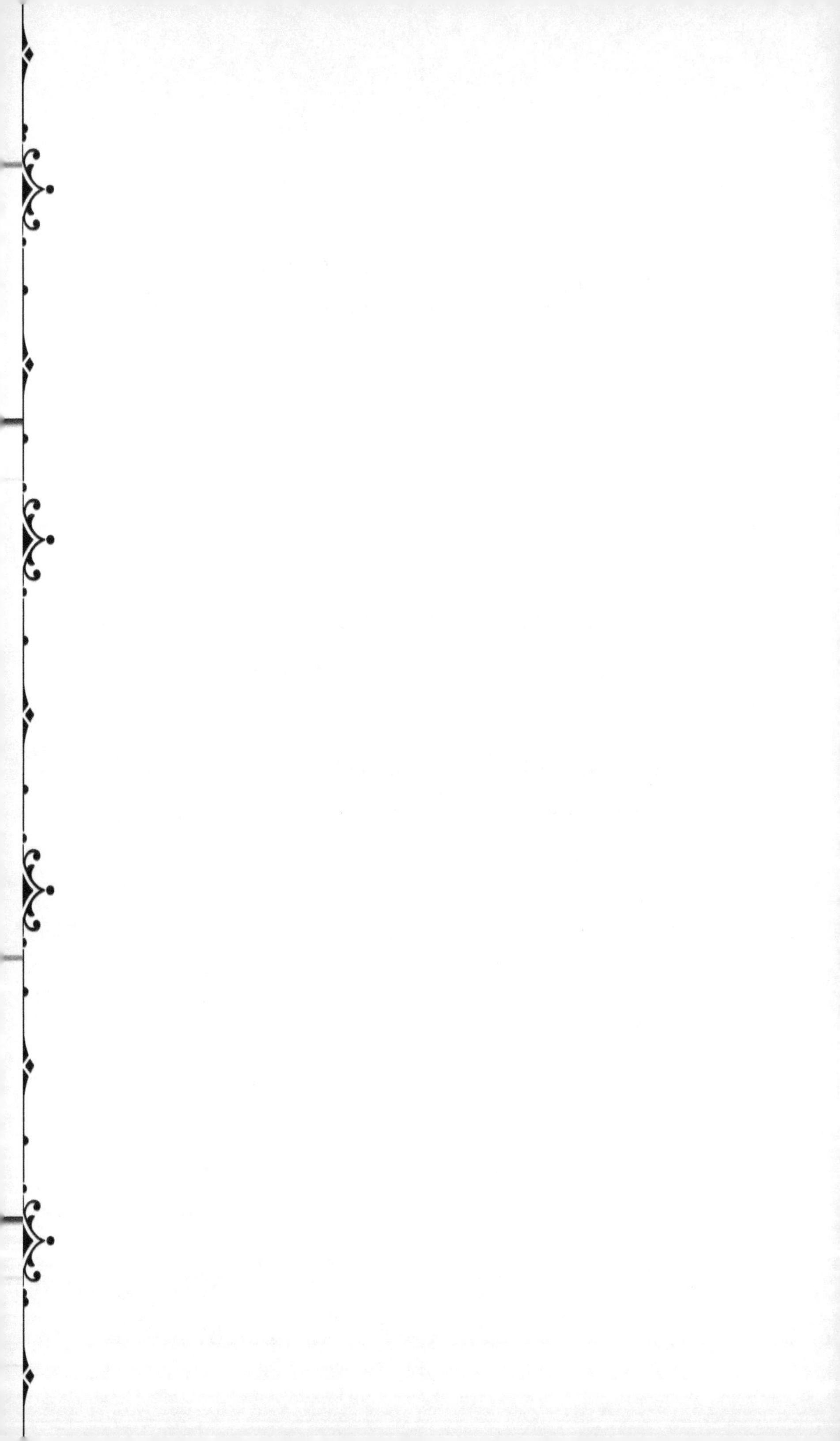

About the Author

Raised in a small town in the heart of Louisiana's Cajun Country, C. A. Varian spent most of her childhood fishing, crabbing, and getting sunburnt at the beach. Her love of reading began very young, and she would often compete at school to read enough books to earn prizes.

Graduating with the first of her college degrees as a mother of two in her late twenties, she became a public-school teacher, which is the career she still has today. She teaches special education at a local middle school. As of June 1, 2023, however, she will be writing full time!

Writing became a passion project, and she put out her first novel in 2021, and has continued to publish new novels every few months since then, not slowing down for even a minute.

Married to a retired military officer, she spent many years moving around for his career, but they now live in central Alabama, with her youngest daughter, Arianna. Her oldest daughter, Brianna, is enjoying her happily ever after with her new husband and several pups. C. A. Varian has two Shih Tzus that she considers her children. Boy, Charlie, and girl, Luna, are their mommy's shadows. She also has three cats named Ramses, Simba, and Cookie.